AF126590

THE TITANIC TUNNEL

Glen Blackwell

Cover illustration by Anastasiia Frizen

Zoetrope Books

Copyright © 2022 Glen Blackwell

Published by Zoetrope Books 2022
Suffolk, England

All rights reserved

A CIP catalogue record for this book is available from the British Library

ISBN : 978-1-8383252-4-4

www.zoetropebooks.com

For Kate and Leo

Thank you for the idea

School Trip

The coach slowly moved forward, clanking over the ramp which led off the ferry and onto the worn concrete of the terminal. As the driver carefully negotiated the route to the exit, the noise level from the children on board increased with their excitement. It was late afternoon, and the school party were on the final leg of their journey from London. They were in their first year at high school and had come on a trip to Belfast to see where Titanic had been built, and to visit the museum dedicated to it.

'Wow - look at that!' Jack said, nudging Emmie. They were now driving through the city centre on the way to their hotel and were grateful that it was only a short ride from the port.

'Cool!' replied Emmie, looking up and noticing the large yellow shipyard cranes for the first time. 'Are they the cranes which were used to build Titanic?'

'No, I think they might be more modern than that,' Jack answered, running a hand through his short orange hair. 'Whenever I've seen pictures of Titanic being built, it was always covered in scaffolding.'

The pair sat back in their seats, heads turned to the side and eyes fixed on the developing views through the window. They had travelled by road to Liverpool, then taken a ferry across the Irish Sea to Belfast. The sea had been quite calm, but Emmie had still felt seasick on the short voyage. She hadn't been on the open sea before, and the gut-wrenching sensation wasn't something she was looking forward to repeating on their way home.

Jack idly traced out the shape of the big cranes on the window alongside him and then stared with interest as a large metal and glass structure came into view.

'That's the Titanic museum,' explained Emmie, 'look, there's a huge metal sculpture of the name outside.' They both stared in awe at the sharply angled building which, with its four-pointed corners, looked a bit like a star.

'It's been a fairly normal journey,' joked Jack, 'not the most adventurous bus trip we've ever had...'

The previous autumn, Jack and Emmie had been on their usual bus journey home from school and had somehow stumbled back in time to 1940. Experiencing the London Blitz first-hand had given them a unique insight into what life was like for people at the time, but how it had happened, and why to them, was still a mystery. They'd talked endlessly about it to each other but couldn't come up with any plausible reason.

'Were you nervous before we came away?' Emmie asked him.

'What - in case we got stuck somewhere and couldn't get back, you mean?' Jack replied. His face became more serious now - it had been an amazing adventure going back in time, but the constant worry about how and if they might get home again had taken a toll, especially on him.

'I think getting home was more luck than anything else,' Emmie admitted. 'I can't imagine we'll get that chance again but, if we do, we might not be so lucky this time.'

*

The bus pulled up outside a curved building - snapping them out of their conversation. It was set back from the road and rose majestically on pillars at one end to give the impression of floating in the air. 'Ok, everyone - time to get off,' announced their teacher, Mr Hughes. The children all stood up, talking animatedly as they pulled their day bags out of the overhead storage area. 'Quietly please - follow me.' Mr Hughes led the way along the aisle of the coach and down the front steps.

As Emmie stepped onto the pavement, the first sensation she felt was the salty tang of the sea air. Although they were in the middle of a city, they were also very close to the waterside, and this body of water led directly to the sea. A few seagulls flapped around, circling and calling to each other. Emmie looked up apprehensively - 'I hope I don't get anything unpleasant landing on my head,' she said quietly to Jack.

'I'm starving,' he replied, excited to have arrived and not really listening to his friend's comment. 'It's been ages since that cheese and pickle sandwich on the boat...' Emmie rolled her eyes in response - that was typical Jack, always thinking about his stomach.

The coach driver had opened up the big storage lockers under the bus and was handing out cases, reading each name tag out loud, before scanning the group to see who was coming forward. 'Emmie Langford,' he called, lifting a dark grey suitcase with wheels and holding it up.

Emmie put her hand up and eased through the group of children, her dark plaits swinging as she walked. 'Thanks,' she said, reaching out for the handle. As she wheeled the case back towards the line of children who had collected their luggage and were forming up to enter the hotel, she heard Jack's name being called over her shoulder. A moment later, the coach driver repeated it, louder this time.

'Uh, sorry - that's me,' called Jack. He had been trying to play a quick game of Top Trumps with some of the other boys and had totally missed the driver calling him. A little red in the face at being caught out, he retrieved his case and joined the line a few places behind Emmie.

She grinned at him and pulled a face - 'Wakey wakey, Jack!' At that moment, the queue began to move into the hotel reception - Mr Hughes having come back with a large stack of room keys.

'Right, everyone - take a key, drop your case in your room and we'll meet here again in 15 minutes,' he instructed. 'We can go for a walk and see what we'll be exploring tomorrow.'

*

As he closed the pale wooden door of his room, Jack looked to his right and saw Emmie doing the same. She had her school uniform jacket on over a white blouse. 'I guess it might be a bit cool outside,' he said, and quickly went back into his room to collect his own jacket.

They filed out of the main hotel door, Mr Hughes checking that everyone was present and then leading the group along the road towards the dockyard. He pointed out sights in the distance which they would visit the next day - the large, yellow cranes, the museum and the dry dock - where he told them that Titanic and her sister ship Olympic were built. The enthusiastic man was both their form tutor and history teacher, and he had managed to weave a Titanic theme through most of their subjects this term.

The school party paused to look out over the flat landscape, towards the dry dock. It didn't look much from here, but Mr Hughes was explaining that it held the equivalent of 180 swimming pools of water and could be pumped dry in just an hour and a half.

'Did they build the whole ship in there?' a boy at the front asked the teacher.

Mr Hughes smiled - this was his favourite subject, and he could talk for hours on it. 'Well, yes,' he started, 'the hull - or the bottom part - of the ship was built on a slipway and then it was launched into the water. It would be floated into the dry dock, which could then be drained, to finish the inside and the taller parts, like the funnels.'

'How did they get it into the water, sir?' the boy replied, 'it must have been really heavy.'

'Soap,' answered Mr Hughes. 'Yes, really,' he went on, noticing the rows of disbelieving faces in front of him. 'Apparently, over twenty tons of soap and animal fat were spread on the slipway to make it slippery enough for Titanic to slide into the water.'

'How fast could it go?' piped up a girl on the other side of the group, waving her hand in the air at the same time.

'I believe the top speed was 23 knots,' came the answer, 'that's about 26 miles per hour. It doesn't sound fast but it really is for something that huge. Titanic had four enormous funnels to take the smoke and steam away from the engine room - generally more funnels meant more power and speed.'

Emmie gazed around her as she listened - behind them was a row of derelict-looking warehouse buildings. They were constructed of red brick and, tucked away at the end, was a small glass-fronted shop with faded blue paintwork. She watched as a man approached, carrying a black case which he set down outside the shop and opened to take out a violin. He arranged the case, still open and facing outwards, in front of him and began to play a haunting tune.

Captivated by this, Emmie tugged Jack's arm and pointed towards the busker. The man turned and smiled at them as he continued his melody. 'Come on,' she said, 'let's go and have a look.'

Jack looked doubtful - 'Are you sure?' he whispered, 'Mr Hughes will wonder where we've gone.'

'It's ok, we'll only be a moment,' Emmie assured him. 'There's something unusual about this. What's so special about that shop for the busker to have chosen to play outside it? There's no-one but us around after all.' The music wormed its way into her ears and, as she turned to look back at the rest of the group, she couldn't hear Mr Hughes at all - in fact, if she didn't know better, she would have said that the rest of the group had turned into statues.

Pulling Jack by the arm again, they got closer and saw that the shop was shut. Just visible through the peeling paint, they could make out stencilled letters above the window. Emmie squinted to read the aged script - 'White something,' she said. 'White Star... Line?'

Jack let out a low whistle - 'White Star Line were the company who owned Titanic,' he said, turning to Emmie. The busker seemed to hear this too as they saw him nod as Jack spoke. He was dressed formally - wearing a dinner suit and a dark overcoat which hung open. As the man continued to play, Jack noticed some steps next to the shop, leading down into a small tunnel.

Emmie saw his gaze - 'I don't know, Jack,' she hesitated. 'You remember what happened last time we saw a strange blue shop...' Jack didn't need reminding - suddenly finding themselves in 1940 was something neither of them was ever likely to forget.

'We got back though, didn't we? No-one even noticed we'd been away - it was like time had stood still.' Despite the earlier conversation, Jack was feeling bullish about their chance to have another adventure. 'Anyway, not every blue shop leads to a time portal - I've been into loads since, and nothing has happened.'

Emmie was keen to explore too - feeling that she had to ask the sensible questions first though, as Jack was quite impulsive. In their last adventure, he had run headlong into everything, treating it like a game, before coming down to earth with a bang when reality set in. That said, life had definitely been boring since they had returned home. You couldn't travel back in time without being curious about any chance to have another go. The tunnel was probably just going to take them into an empty cellar, but the possible connection with White Star Line, and therefore maybe Titanic, was just too much to pass up.

Out of nowhere, a ship's foghorn sounded loudly, making the pair jump. Jack turned to Emmie - 'That must be a sign - there aren't any ships out there on the water - look...'

The Tunnel

Finally making up her mind, Emmie stepped towards the tunnel entrance, pausing to look up at the elaborate stone arch she had noticed above it. It seemed out of place compared to the run-down buildings on either side - there was a bit of faded glamour in the architecture, and she was intrigued to find out what lay beyond. With Jack following her, she walked down the steps slowly - her hand stroking the rough texture of the brickwork.

'It smells quite bad, doesn't it?' said Emmie, as her eyes adjusted to the gloom. There was a damp, musty aroma in the air and she didn't imagine that anyone else had been through here in a long time. As they rounded a curve in the tunnel, and the daylight coming from behind them faded further, Emmie glanced at Jack. He was chewing his lip - a sure sign that he was anxious. She reached for his hand and gave it a gentle squeeze. 'Not scared, are you?' she teased, smiling as he as he screwed up his face at her in response.

'Anyway, it's getting lighter up ahead - we must be nearly there.'

They passed through an open doorway, then Emmie suddenly stumbled and reached out for the wall to steady herself. Jack stopped, then he too felt his legs almost give way and grabbed onto Emmie. 'What's happening?' he stammered, 'I don't like this...'

'It's like the floor just moved,' answered Emmie. They looked at each other in the semi-darkness - there was a definite swaying sensation as they stood together in the damp space. 'It must just be because it's so gloomy down here - tricking our balance maybe,' Emmie wondered aloud. She felt a sudden wave of nausea in her stomach, taking her mind back to the ferry crossing earlier. 'Just give me a moment?' she said, still leaning against the wall for support.

The sick feeling eased, and they carried on - curiosity getting the better of them. As they reached the source of the light, the pair noticed that it was shining around a heavy looking wooden door which stood ajar. Jack reached for the handle, intending to pull it open.

'Wait a minute,' whispered Emmie, placing a finger to her lips and stepping forward. She peered around the door, then stepped back in surprise, her mouth wide open.

'What is it?' Jack whispered back, craning his head for a look. Emmie was still staring through the gap as Jack leaned around her and studied the scene beyond. 'What is that...?' he managed, almost as speechless as his friend.

As she tried to recover herself, Emmie stepped forward again and stared. What lay past the door was a large, elaborate space, with a grand wooden staircase in the centre. Sweeping balustrades and ornately carved decoration curved upwards, and there was a constant stream of smartly dressed people ascending and descending. A perfumed aroma wafted through the door, contrasting with the damp smell in the tunnel.

Emmie recoiled in horror as a lady in a purple dress and matching hat passed closely by and seemed to make eye contact with her, bumping into Jack in the process.

'Careful!' he said, almost forgetting that they were trying to be quiet.

'Sorry,' she replied, 'I'm sure that woman saw us peeking though.'

There was a general burble of conversation from the other side of the door, as people made their way past.

Some of the voices were more constant though, as if their owners were right outside.

'Did you see Queenstown this morning?' enquired one voice, close enough that they almost felt the speaker must be next to them. 'That's the last piece of land this side of the Atlantic.' There was a muffled answer which sounded negative, and then the first voice spoke again - 'I heard we took on another hundred or so passengers - steerage mostly, so they won't be bothering us.'

The second person replied more clearly this time - 'Going to America in the hope of a better life, I suppose. I noticed us drop anchor for a few hours and wondered why - it looked like we were still at sea though.'

'The berth is a couple of miles offshore - I heard one of the crew mention it. You could see the passengers coming aboard bobbing about in little boats on the way over.'

'Rather them than me - I'm much happier in a liner than a little boat.'

Jack looked at Emmie - 'Queenstown?' he said, 'where's that?' They had both studied Titanic extensively over the past few weeks, but Jack hadn't recalled that detail.

'Southern Ireland, I think,' Emmie replied, 'I'm pretty sure I read it was the last passenger stop.' She thought again for a moment - 'It was renamed in the 1920's, so isn't on any of today's maps - that's probably why you didn't recognise it.'

'Who are they, and what are they doing down here?' Jack asked after a pause. The size of the space beyond the door seemed much bigger than they imagined a cellar could be - it didn't really make any sense. Another second or two passed, and then an uncomfortable thought hit him - 'Is that...? No, it can't be...'

'Surely it hasn't happened again...' Emmie said slowly in reply. She peered around the door for another look - this time braving a gentle tug to widen the gap slightly. The door silently obliged, opening up a further sliver of the view beyond. Standing to the left of the staircase were groups of tables and chairs, set out in a café style, and halfway up the stairs was a large wooden carving which housed an elaborate clock. Emmie stared at it and could just make out the immortal words - RMS Titanic - stencilled on the clock face. She stepped back again and nodded slowly at Jack.

'Let's get out of here,' he tugged her arm desperately; his enthusiasm having evaporated. Jack had been the more despondent of the friends when they had found themselves stranded in the Blitz, and he wasn't about to risk not getting home again. It still seemed unbelievable that people could travel back in time, but there wasn't a better explanation for what was happening to them.

Emmie found herself walking quickly back along the tunnel behind Jack - her mind in turmoil. 'Hold on a minute,' she hissed as they rounded the corner and could see the entrance once more. 'It's Titanic - aren't you curious? No one alive today has seen it like that.'

'No.' The reply was immediate. Jack's head was down, but he had stopped and then slowly turned back to face her. His lip was quivering, and Emmie could see that he was really scared at the prospect of the unknown - yet something was drawing her back along the tunnel just as strongly as the busker's music had prompted her to investigate in the first place.

'Just another quick peek?' begged Emmie, looking Jack right in the eye. 'We'll never get this chance again - you know that. We'll just have a quick look and then come straight back.'

Jack looked away - 'What if we get stuck again?'

'It's just an open door,' came the reply. 'Once we've explored, we can turn around and come back through it.'

Screwing his eyes up, Jack nodded, and Emmie gave him a big grin. 'Come on,' she said, linking arms with him and starting back towards the door, 'it's going to be amazing!'

SLAM! The sudden noise behind them made the pair jump, echoing in the enclosed space. 'What was that?!' cried Jack, turning in the direction of the sound.

*

They raced back along the uneven floor, stopping abruptly at the previously open doorway in the middle of the tunnel. Their path was now blocked by another stout wooden door - a thin dust cloud hanging in the air and just visible in the half-light of the tunnel.

Jack grabbed at the handle, fumbling to get it open in his rising panic. At first, the rusty mechanism resisted his tugging, then abruptly relented - pitching Jack backwards onto the floor. He grunted, then got to his feet, peering curiously at the now open door. 'Huh?' he said, 'what's that?' He reached out to touch the object on the other side of the doorway. It was dark and smooth, and appeared larger than the door opening itself. There seemed to be some sort of circular hole in the middle too. He ran his fingers along the object slowly, lifting them over some raised bumps in a neat line, before looking back at Emmie.

'It's metal...' he said, confusion in his voice. 'What is it though? It wasn't there before...' Then it dawned on him - the round porthole and line of rivets meant they were looking at the metal plates making up the side of a ship...

'What's going on?!' cried Jack in alarm. 'A minute ago, we were talking about walking through an open door and now we're already stuck inside the ship?' His voice had become higher as he spoke, and Emmie could see him chewing his lip again.

She walked over to the doorway and gently traced a finger across the metal plate, as Jack had done. Rapping her knuckles on it confirmed that it was both metal and very large, as the plate gave a dull echo, rather than a ringing noise. Trying to keep calm, Emmie considered their options which, at this point, seemed rather limited.

'I don't think we're going to get out this way,' she said, stating the obvious and noticing Jack's face fall even further. 'I reckon our best, and probably only, choice is to go through that door and find another way out.'

'What? Onto Titanic?' Jack couldn't believe he was hearing this - it had been one thing to suggest an adventure with an easy exit route back, but this was totally different. 'I want to go home,' he said firmly.

'Well, what's your idea then?' asked Emmie - her concern giving way to a feeling of frustration. Jack was being ridiculous - there wasn't another option as far as she could see.

As she watched, his face crumpled, and her emotions turned once again - this time to pity. Emmie put a comforting arm around her friend and turned him around to face the door into the ship. 'Be brave, Jack,' she said, 'we can do this - just got to be smart about it.' Sighing, he allowed her to lead him back towards the door and the crack of light shining around it.

*

It was Emmie's turn to reach for the handle this time. As she swung the door open, she noticed a thick curtain covering part of the opening and pulled them both behind it. As the pair peeked out, Emmie realised that there was no one on the staircase now and the room seemed deserted. 'Ready to find a way out?' she asked quietly.

Jack still looked unsure but, before he could answer, Emmie had slipped out from behind the curtain and walked quickly across to the grand staircase. She looked up at the landing above, paused for a moment and then started up the stairs, scanning the room around her as she ascended. It was quiet on the landing above, as the stairs rose to their final level and an ornate glass dome towered over the room.

'Emmie!' Jack hissed urgently, but it was clear that she couldn't hear him. He looked out from behind the curtain again and then stepped forward, intending to follow her.

'Baxter! What are you doing up here?!' came a man's voice from his right, and he felt a strong hand clamp onto his shoulder. 'Get back into the kitchen, now!' Jack flinched and looked at the man in alarm - who was he and where had he come from? He wore a dark uniform with shiny buttons on it and was a good head taller than Jack himself. The man gave him a little push and indicated a door at the end of the room in the direction which he'd appeared from.

'But—' Jack began and was immediately cut off.

'No arguments, boy. You've got a job to do - there's to be no slacking off and this area is out of bounds to kitchen staff anyway.'

Jack tried to wriggle free of the man's grip, but he squeezed more firmly. 'Ouch!' he cried, 'that hurts!' One look at the man's face told Jack that he meant business, and his shoulders slumped in defeat.

As he reluctantly allowed himself to be steered towards the kitchen, Jack looked up and caught sight of Emmie staring in horror at the scene below her. She just about managed to mouth 'Meet me here later? When you can...' as he was frogmarched underneath where she stood and disappeared from sight.

Where's Jack?

Emmie stifled a sob as she looked around the room below her, in the vain hope that Jack would somehow reappear. She could just about hear his footsteps, and those of the man who had bundled him off, receding into the distance. The sound died away, and the space was silent once more.

This was going from bad to worse - first they were stuck, and now they'd got separated. Emmie knew she needed to find Jack quickly - they stood a much better chance of working out how to get home if they both put their minds to it.

She looked down at her watch, wondering how much time had passed already, and blinked in surprise when she read the face - 24:00. 'What's that?' she muttered to herself - there wasn't a twenty-four o'clock... The numbers didn't seem to be moving either - maybe she had knocked it somehow? It was doing nothing to dispel the odd sensation that she felt at being stuck on board a doomed ship, 110 years in the past though.

Pulling herself together and glancing down, Emmie stared at the groups of chairs and tables either side of the staircase, wondering where everyone had gone. When they had first peered around the door, the room was bustling, with people chatting at tables and moving up and down the stairs - now it was eerily empty.

Cautiously, she moved down the staircase, one hand on the smooth banister, playing over in her mind the likelihood of this all being real. It certainly felt like it was - she couldn't work out how else the interior of a huge ship could appear to fit in a small cellar. As she reached the bottom, she listened again to see if she could hear anyone approaching. It was still totally silent.

She turned to face the same way that Jack had disappeared - the room ended with a heavily panelled set of double doors, complete with shiny brass handles. The doors were closed, and Emmie nervously reached for the handle of the right-hand door, turning it gently. As she opened it, a burble of conversation met her ears, and Emmie found herself looking into a restaurant which appeared to be full of diners. She quietly closed the door again and retreated back to the stairs - not ready to encounter any of the passengers yet. At least that helped explain why there was suddenly no-one around - it must be mealtime.

There had been a door leading to the outside on the deck above, and she now climbed the staircase to reach it. As she emerged, she saw a covered deck extending a long way to both the left and right, with rows of deckchairs neatly stacked. There were unglazed window openings along some of its length and, if there had been any doubt about the reality of where they were, this was dispelled by both the salty sea air and the waves stretching as far as the eye could see.

Emmie crossed the deck and grabbed onto the edge of the nearest window opening to steady herself. Now she was outside and could see the horizon, she could sense the motion of the sea and also noticed a steady hum from what she imagined to be the ship's engines. She waited for a moment in case the nausea from earlier returned, but the ship was so stable that it seemed to have passed.

It was cold out on the deck and Emmie pulled her school blazer tight around her. She had been able to tell from the brief glance into the restaurant that it stretched back along the ship, so decided to head towards the rear, noticing a room to her left with windows facing out onto the deck. As she peered through the first window, she could see tables and chairs arranged together and a few people sitting at them. Almost involuntarily, she quickened her pace, only daring to lift her head and look again when she was past the room.

Reaching a barrier, where the rail curved away from the side and stopped her going any further, Emmie saw that there were some cranes and another deck below where she stood. This ship was enormous - she had walked less than half the length of it and could barely see where she had come from. Turning back, Emmie could see a small staircase up ahead and climbed it. She emerged onto what looked like the top level of the ship, complete with rows of shiny white lifeboats sitting on their derricks.

Looking to her left, in the direction Jack had gone, Emmie noticed a sign further along the deck announcing in black painted letters - '2nd Class Promenade'. 'I guess this must be 1st class, then,' she murmured to herself. She thought it unlikely that the kitchen would be in the 1st class part of the ship, confirming her plan to head towards the rear.

At the far end of this deck, there was a covered staircase leading downwards, and Emmie cautiously descended. At the first landing, not quite sure what to do next, she emerged onto the deck and looked around - the staircase carried on down and there was also a large room with its door opposite the stairs. Trying the door handle, Emmie was immediately beaten back by a fug of smoke. She shut the door hurriedly, but not before observing a number of people inside, and the hum of conversation. She began to feel a little relieved at seeing more people, yet uncomfortable as their first interaction on Titanic had been so shocking. Looking down at her watch again, she saw that it still stubbornly read 24:00, and would be no use for telling her how long they had been on board for.

There was no way she wanted to go back into the smoking room - the sign on the door advertised it as such - so she turned and started to go down the stairs. The décor was definitely less grand on this staircase - although it was still made of wood, there were no carvings, and the overall effect was a lot simpler.

Reaching the next landing, Emmie paused and could feel a sense of dread washing over her. The ship was huge, and finding Jack wasn't going to be easy. Giving herself a minute, she smiled politely as a man walked past her, whilst trying to quell the twisting knot in her stomach. The faint smell of food drifted up from the deck below and caught her attention - food should equal kitchen, right?

She carried on down the stairs and saw that there was a queue of people waiting at the bottom, snaking past the landing and back towards rows of narrow cabin doors. A few people stared at her and she wondered if she stood out a bit in her school uniform. Before she had time to think any further, there was a commotion further up the queue and a teenage boy came running past her, accompanied by some angry shouts. She looked to her right and saw a red-faced man in what she took to be a waiter's uniform shaking his fist angrily at the rapidly retreating boy.

'Thieving little so and so - he doesn't belong up here,' sniffed a lady standing opposite her, huffily.

'Quite so, dear,' replied the man to her side. 'They should lock those doors between the decks.'

Deciding that this queue of passengers, with their intolerance for outsiders, might not be the best place to be, Emmie carried on down the stairs, descending two further decks and feeling increasingly despondent. As she reached the bottom, she saw a sign announcing that this was F deck and wondered exactly how many decks the giant ship actually had.

There was a lot less effort in design on this deck, Emmie noticed. The wood had largely given way to metal - everything from the handrails to the walls themselves were bare, painted steel. There was a small notice stencilled below the F deck sign, pointing to the 3rd class dining room to her right. Emmie smiled to herself and headed in that direction - the smell of cooking unmistakeably wafting down the corridor towards her. Even if she didn't find the kitchen along here, there would still be a chance to grab some food. The twisted stomach feeling had passed, and despite her worried state she hadn't realised how hungry she was - having last eaten on the ferry from Liverpool earlier that day.

As she turned a corner, Emmie noticed the ever-present hum of the ship's engines becoming louder. It seemed to be coming from behind the wall to her right and, when she reached her fingers out to touch it, she could feel gentle vibrations. Continuing along the corridor, she suddenly came up against the end of another queue. This one was a lot shorter and the people in it were dressed less formally. Immediately, she felt more relaxed, though still a bit conscious of her school uniform. She took her blazer off and tucked it under her arm - the white blouse looking less out of place.

*

After what seemed like an eternity, Emmie found herself approaching the serving area to the left of the main dining space. There was a long, low hatch with a counter set in it - behind which were a line of serving staff ready to fill a plate for you. Emmie reached the end of the counter and watched a plate get handed along the line for the woman in front of her - first some slices of roast beef, then a scoop of boiled potatoes and a generous serving of sweetcorn. At the end, a small man with greying hair and a permanently fixed smile handed over the plate. As she approached the counter, she grabbed a couple of bread rolls and put them onto the plate which was offered to her. 'Nothing else?' asked the man, indicating the hot food.

'No thanks, I'm fine' she said, eager to get on with finding Jack.

That was the easy part done - now to find somewhere to sit, as she couldn't really wander around the ship eating without looking out of place. Emmie turned and surveyed the packed room. At this end, the tables were filled with men, and she could see beyond a bulkhead running down the centre of the room, that the space beyond had family groups seated. Heading through the bulkhead it was apparent that there were very few empty seats in either section and she paused, unsure how to engage in conversation with the other passengers. Aware of people moving behind her and the need to sit down, Emmie headed for a corner at the back of the room, where a large family sat with two empty seats at the end of their table.

Emmie smiled at them as she put her plate down. The blazer was still tucked under her arm, and she loosely draped it across the back of the chair before sitting down. Aside of the parents, there were three older girls, a girl around Emmie's age wearing a pretty dress, and a boy who looked slightly younger. The family had obviously almost finished eating and, before she had time to worry about what she might say to them, they rose and left through a door on the opposite side to where Emmie had entered. As they went, the younger girl turned to look at her, a shy smile on her face.

The family were quickly replaced by another group who sat down alongside Emmie. 'Are you on your own?' asked the man who seated himself next to her. His wife looked concernedly in her direction too.

'No, my family came in earlier,' she replied quickly. 'I wasn't hungry before.' Feeling reluctant to get involved in further conversation with someone who had questioned whether she was alone spurred Emmie on to finish her rolls quickly. 'Goodbye,' she said politely, rising from the table with her plate in hand and walking purposefully away.

'Wait - you've forgotten your jacket,' the man called.

Emmie stopped and sighed to herself - so much for avoiding attention! She turned and smiled graciously, walking back over to the table and taking the offered garment. 'Thank you - very kind,' she responded, hoping that she would make a cleaner escape this time around.

*

Leaving the dining room, Emmie immediately found herself climbing a staircase and emerging into a wide corridor, which appeared be in use by crew members and passengers alike.

Emmie turned left and started to walk towards the back of the ship, in an effort to locate the kitchen where she hoped that Jack would be. It felt logical that the kitchen must be close to the dining room - either this one or the 2nd class one that she had passed earlier. Carrying on along the corridor, she turned this way and that, trying to avoid the constant stream of people moving in both directions.

Stepping out to avoid an open door, she half-tripped over a sack which had been left propped up against the wall. Stumbling to regain her balance, Emmie spun around - she felt suddenly disorientated and pressed herself into a small alcove in the grey passage wall. Staring wildly around, she couldn't remember which way she had come from - everything looked the same on this part of the ship. She forced herself to breathe slowly and, after a few moments, a sense of perspective started to return. This was just panic, she told herself, and it wasn't surprising, given the circumstances.

She looked each way in turn, noticing that the door she had stepped out to avoid was still open, and was able to work out the right way to go. Continuing along the corridor, she passed another open doorway and was distracted from her thoughts by the sound of someone crying. She stopped and turned around, peering into the relative gloom of the small room in front of her. At the back, sitting on the ground and with her knees drawn up in front of her, was the girl who had smiled at her in the dining room earlier. She was sobbing and, as she looked up, Emmie could see that her eyes were red from crying.

'What's the matter?' Emmie asked gently, crouching down beside the girl.

'My brothers...' she replied between loud sobs, 'they're missing!'

The Vanishing Room

'What do you mean?' said Emmie, reaching out and placing her hand gently on the girl's arm.

She looked up - 'We haven't seen them since breakfast time. Father's searched all over the ship, well - the bits we're allowed in anyway.' Welling up again, she said through her tears - 'I'm so worried about them.'

'Did they run off?' asked Emmie. 'Is it something they do often?'

'They slipped away earlier and went through a door into a tiny room,' she sniffed. 'I was following them, and the door only closed for a second, but when it opened, they had vanished.'

Emmie gave the girl's arm a squeeze and smiled at her - 'I'm sure they'll turn up - they've probably just lost track of time. What's your name anyway?'

'Mary. Mary Kelly,' replied the girl, wiping her face with her hand.

'Well, I'm Emmie - Emmie Langford. It's nice to meet you.' She paused for a moment - 'What do your brothers look like?'

'Patrick is a bit shorter than me - he's got brown hair, and John is up to his shoulder,' Mary explained. 'John has fair hair but is always wearing a cap so you wouldn't really notice.'

Emmie was thinking about how anyone could vanish inside a tiny room. 'Might they have been exploring on some of the higher decks?' she enquired gently.

Mary's face paled - 'Oh, I hope not - we'd be in all kinds of trouble if they were found up there.' She started to sob again and patted her pocket for a handkerchief.

'Why would you be in trouble?' Emmie was confused about how the rules of the ship worked.

'We're 3rd class passengers, you see,' Mary continued, 'we're not allowed in any of the same areas as the higher-class passengers. Something to do with disease apparently.'

Emmie was horrified - was Mary really telling her that 3rd class passengers were assumed to be carrying disease?

Mary must have noticed Emmie's expression and quickly added - 'Father says it's an immigration rule - if they keep groups of people separate, then any diseases that might get brought onto the ship are contained and don't spread everywhere.' She thought for a moment and then continued - 'Are you from one of the upper decks then? Is that why you didn't know?'

Emmie wasn't sure how to respond to this - she hadn't expected a challenge as to why she was there this soon. Thinking she'd have to be more careful with what she said in future, Emmie attempted a confident tone - 'I'm on the way to my dad in New York - he's meeting me when the ship docks.'

'Are you on your own then?' continued Mary.

'Yes - I've got one of the stewards keeping an eye on me but I'm travelling on my own,' explained Emmie. 'I'm on D deck,' she concluded - hoping that this sounded plausible to the girl.

'Aren't you worried about getting into trouble for being down here?'

'I won't tell if you don't,' Emmie said quietly, putting her finger to her lips to emphasise the point. 'Anyway, I can't help you look for your brothers if I'm not down here.'

Mary's face brightened at this - 'Oh, would you?' she exclaimed happily, 'that would be so kind.'

Emmie stood up, offering her hand to Mary, who took it gratefully. 'Where first?' she asked, 'shall we start with the little room your brothers went into?'

Mary led Emmie along the wide corridor and down some steps at the end. They then doubled back and stopped outside some lift doors, set within a stairwell. 'That's the room,' she said, pointing at the lift.

Emmie looked back at her in confusion - 'that's a lift...'

'A what?'

Suddenly Emmie understood, putting a hand to her mouth to stifle a grin. It made sense now - a small room which someone appeared to vanish from... She wasn't sure how to explain this concept to Mary, who had obviously never seen such a thing before. 'Follow me,' she said, walking over to the lift door and pressing the illuminated button.

'Be careful!' warned Mary, not wanting to lose her new friend too.

The door slid open to reveal a young boy in a smart uniform jacket. He smiled at them, and Emmie stepped inside, holding her hand out for Mary to join her.

Mary's face betrayed the conflict which she must have been feeling - she wanted to know where her brothers were but was terrified of vanishing too.

'Come on, it's ok,' called Emmie, 'you'll love it.'

The other girl slowly walked over to the lift and stepped inside, her eyes scanning the interior suspiciously. 'Where did they go?' she asked, 'there's no other door...'

'Up one, please,' Emmie said to the lift boy, then took Mary's hand. She watched with barely suppressed amusement as the girl's eyes nearly popped out of her head when the lift car started to move. Almost as soon as they had started, the lift stopped again, and the door slid open.

Emmie gently led Mary out into the lobby area in front of the lift. 'Well?' she asked, 'what did you think of that?'

Mary's mouth moved but, to begin with, no words came out. When she had collected herself, she managed to ask, 'Did we just go up in that?'

Nodding, Emmie explained that Patrick and John had most likely done the same thing and enjoyed their first ride in a lift.

'But where are they now?' said Mary.

'Maybe they rode it all the way to the top?'

'How are we going to look up there?' Mary wondered out loud. 'I'll be in big trouble if I get caught.'

'Big trouble from who?' asked Emmie. 'What's the worst that could happen? It's not like they're going to make you get off the ship.'

'My father... for one,' replied Mary, 'he's a stickler for the rules, and he won't want any of us drawing attention to ourselves. This is life changing for our family and getting sent back rather than going to America would be terrible.'

Emmie nodded, trying to understand how much it must mean to Mary to be able to start a new life halfway around the world. 'We just need to blend in,' she explained, 'then no-one will think we're not meant to be there.' She looked at Mary, who was wearing a floral dress with a knitted shawl around her shoulders. The dress would be fine on its own, but the shawl would have to go. 'Tell you what,' she suggested, 'why don't we go via your cabin, put your shawl back and do something different with your hair?'

Mary agreed eagerly, leading the way back down the stairs to where they had entered the lift. 'It's not along there,' she tugged Emmie's arm, guiding her in the other direction. 'We're quite near the back of the ship.'

As they worked their way around the rabbit warren of narrow passageways on F deck, Emmie could hear raised voices coming from a few of the cabins. 'It can be a bit noisy down here sometimes,' Mary said apologetically. They reached a door set into the corner of the passage - it was a gunmetal grey colour, like everything on this deck. 'Here we are - I think Mother was having a lay down, so I'll go and put my shawl away quickly.' Mary opened the door and quietly closed it behind her. When she emerged a few minutes later, she was pinning her hair up into a bun on the top of her head - 'I thought this might help too.'

Emmie smiled encouragingly and took Mary's hand in hers. They retraced their steps to the deck above and walked along the corridor to the stairwell with the lift in. 'Just act like you're meant to be here,' Emmie whispered as they emerged from the stairs at the next landing. 'I think we should explore the area around these stairs on each deck first. Hopefully the boys haven't gone far.' They found themselves walking towards the 2nd class dining room - the food smell from earlier had gone and there was no queue snaking out from the doorway. The door to the dining room was closed, and it was very quiet in this part of the ship.

As they reached the door, Emmie put out a hand to push it open. The door silently swung inwards and revealed a large space the full width of the ship, filled with rows of tables, each topped with white tablecloths. In contrast to the spartan layout of the 3rd class dining room, rows of carved wooden chairs lined either side of the tables, and elaborate wooden panelling covered the walls. The room was dimly lit - the only natural light coming from the windows at either side of the ship, and none of the ceiling lights being on.

'Patrick? John?' called Mary quietly, as they slipped inside the dining room. There was no reply and, after a quick walk across the room, it was obvious that there was no-one else about. There were two sets of doors at the far end, and on impulse, Emmie tugged the first one open - seeing that it led onto a staircase going up. She closed it again, then opened the second door -

stopping in shock, she realised that this led into the kitchens. She peered through the gap, scanning the room beyond and trying to see if she could spot Jack. Just as she opened the door a bit further to get a better look, there was an angry shout, and a man came striding in her direction. She shrank back from the door, letting it close just in time to hear a loud clang from the other side as a bolt was slammed home.

Kitchen Drama

'Keep going, Baxter!' said the man sharply under his breath, as he strode along at Jack's shoulder.

'My name isn't—' started Jack, earning himself a growl in reply.

He sneaked a sideways glance as he was led quickly through the restaurant. His captor was wearing a dark uniform of jacket and trousers. He had a neat moustache and was slightly red in the face.

'Where are we going?' Jack tried again. He was still in shock at being propelled so abruptly away from Emmie.

'The kitchen, where you should have been already. If an officer had seen you up here, he'd have had you thrown off the ship!'

Jack swallowed nervously at this point. He opened his mouth to reply but thought better of it - the man looked quite angry still, and Jack didn't fancy annoying him further.

They reached a door and passed through it, out onto a decked area. Jack saw a small sign which read '2nd Class Promenade Deck' and was then almost immediately shoved back inside through another door.

'That's why you can't go off wandering about - there's people to feed,' explained the man, his tone having softened very slightly.

Jack found himself at the top of a double staircase and followed the man down. They descended two flights of stairs, emerging into a small lobby. There were large double doors in front of them, and another dining area was visible through the decorative glass. Behind him was a further door and it was this one which he discovered they were going through.

Beyond the lobby was a narrow corridor, running past numerous storerooms and filled with men and boys carrying provisions. As Jack looked to his right, he saw an enormous stack of bread inside one room and suddenly realised that he was hungry.

'No time for that at the moment,' said the man, leading him further along the corridor and pushing a door open at the end. Jack saw that he was in a large kitchen - an enormous cooking range sat in the middle and took up most of the room, with tables and work surfaces set around the edges. The kitchen was a hive of activity as ingredients were measured and meals prepared. It was noisy - but not with talking - the chatter of mixers and the clash of pans were drowning out any opportunity for conversation.

'Found one of yours upstairs,' the man announced to a tall chef, who was making soup in a huge pan. The chef looked at Jack curiously.

'Really?' His eyes narrowed and then he pointed to a row of hooks in the corner. 'Get yourself an apron and take that jacket off - you should be wearing a white one.'

Jack reached the hooks and saw that there were a variety of aprons and white chef's jackets hanging there. He took his school blazer off and replaced it with a white jacket and clean apron.

'Look lively!' shouted the chef, over the noise of the kitchen.

Jack hurried back over, nervously wondering what was going to happen next. He didn't know how to cook, so this probably wasn't going to go well.

The chef slid a chopping board and knife across the counter to Jack. 'I need twenty onions chopping,' he instructed, 'they're behind you.'

Jack turned around - there was a row of at least thirty sacks of vegetables, their sides rolled down to expose what was inside. He walked over to a sack of large, brown onions and picked two up.

'I haven't got all day,' the chef shouted across to him, 'you'll need to carry more than that.'

Jack sighed and lifted up the hem of his apron in one hand, dropping the onions into it and grabbing at some more. He staggered back across the room, onions threatening to spill out with every movement. Placing them in a pile next to the chopping board, he picked up the knife and started to peel the first onion. By the time he was halfway through, his eyes were streaming, and he could hardly see. Fighting twin emotions of anger and frustration, he gritted his teeth and finished the last onion.

'Twenty,' said the chef, with more than a hint of annoyance, 'not ten.'

Groaning inwardly, Jack repeated the whole exercise, dabbing his eyes on the apron string periodically. When he had finally finished, he put down his knife, rubbed his hands on the apron and risked a quick look around. No-one seemed to be paying him any notice now - the row of chefs to his right were concentrating on their cooking, and there was a constant stream of boys around his age carrying dishes out of a door at the end of the room.

Curious as to where the boys were going, he watched them for a moment and then, realising that the chef who had made him prepare the onions had disappeared, he decided to follow. He picked up a basket of rolls and walked around the counter towards the door, trying to act casually. Looking around, he quickly stuffed a roll into his mouth and furtively chewed it. He kept his head down to mask the eating, and followed a tall, dark-haired boy out of the door. The next room seemed to be a sort of preparation room for food which didn't need cooking, and most of the boys were passing straight through a door ahead of them.

Jack reached the door and gently pushed it open, then almost stopped in shock at the opulence of the room he had entered. There was a gentle buzz of polite conversation coming from all around - people sat at heavy wooden tables, covered in fine white cloths and with an amazing array of crockery and cutlery in front of them. The room itself was painted cream and heavily decorated - the walls were wooden panelled, and the ceiling had an intricate plasterwork pattern woven across it.

He would have stared for longer, rooted to the spot in awe, but for another boy emerging through the door behind him and giving him a little shove as he passed. Jack realised that he was starting to look out of place and hurriedly put his basket of bread down in front of the passengers on a nearby table.

Turning to go back through the door, he couldn't resist one last peek at the grand dining room and was nearly knocked flying by the door opening in front of him.

'This one's out only,' muttered a boy who was carrying a tray of plates, and Jack noticed that there were two doors almost next to each other. He pushed the other one open and allowed himself to breathe a small sigh of relief once he was back inside the preparation area.

Scratching his head absent-mindedly, Jack wondered how he was going to get out of this particular situation. He obviously looked like one of the kitchen workers, and moving about to find Emmie felt like it was going to be more difficult now. It had seemed like a good idea to let her talk him into venturing back onto the ship earlier but now they were stuck and who knows what had happened to Emmie.

'Come along, lad' - a voice snapped Jack out of his thoughts, and he looked up to see an older man in a grubby apron staring at him. 'If you've nothing to do, there's plenty of washing up. Follow me.'

This was getting worse now - Jack hated washing up and, despite the roll he'd eaten, was still feeling hungry. 'What time's tea?' he asked, unsure what kind of reply he was going to get.

The man looked back at him strangely - 'Tea?' he asked, 'do you mean dinner?' Jack nodded -mindful that he would need to be careful with his terminology going forward. 'When they've had theirs - like usual,' the man replied. 'Lots to do before then, though.' He passed through the door back into the kitchen and indicated a row of large sinks in the corner - 'There you go, you can make a start on that.'

Jack surveyed the sink - there were piles and piles of china plates stacked up on the side next to it. His face fell - how was he going to get away to meet Emmie before this lot was done? He looked around, searching for a way out, but the man who had instructed him was still watching.

Turning the taps to fill the sink, Jack looked around for a brush. He noticed that the other boys washing up were all rinsing their plates first, then wiping them in hot water with a bar of soap and a cloth. He picked up the first plate, almost dropped it as it was much lighter than he was expecting, then managed to rinse off the contents, before wiping it with a cloth which the old man appeared at his shoulder with. After he had washed seven or eight plates, Jack was getting really bored, and wondered how he could get out of this job.

As luck would have it, he noticed a younger boy walking back and forth behind him, carrying sacks of flour. He was struggling with the weight of them, and Jack thought he might have found an opportunity.

'Hey,' he called the next time the boy passed by, 'do you want to swap?'

Pausing for a moment and putting down his hessian sack, the boy looked at Jack suspiciously. 'Why would you do that?' he asked.

Jack decided that honesty might be the best option here - 'I'm bored of this, and you look like you're struggling.'

The boy considered his offer, a slight frown on his face as he did so. 'Ok,' he said eventually, 'for a bit.' He stepped over to the sink and started to roll his sleeves up - 'Thanks - I'm Bob.'

Jack picked up the flour, finding it was slightly heavier than he had bargained for. 'I'm Jack,' he replied, 'nice to meet you.' He was hoping that carrying the sack would allow him to move around without being challenged and let him get away from the kitchen.

He passed through the doors at the back of the kitchen, and into the narrow passageway they had walked through earlier. There was a constant procession of people moving through the passage, but no-one took much notice of Jack.

Peering into one of the storerooms, Jack saw that it was full of sacks of flour, just like the one he was carrying. He entered the room and placed his sack down near the door, noticing that a half-full one sat nearby. An idea had popped into his head, and he bent down to pick up the smaller sack - this one would hopefully be a bit easier.

He tested the sack for weight - it was a lot lighter than the one he had brought in - and lifted it onto his shoulder. Leaving the storeroom, he continued down the passage until he came to the stairs which he had been bundled down earlier. Pausing for a moment to listen, he peered up in the direction he wanted to go. It sounded quiet, so he put the sack down and started up the staircase, feeling relieved that he had found a way out of the kitchen.

Turning the corner, up the final flight of steps, the way ahead of him suddenly darkened as a large shadow moved in front of the light coming from the deck above. Jack shrank back against the wall, not quite sure what to do. He was just turning to go back down the stairs when a man appeared, carrying a bottle in each hand.

'What are you doing?' demanded the man, taking in Jack's apron and jacket. 'You shouldn't be up here.'

'Err... I was just... collecting something,' stammered Jack, failing to think of a more plausible explanation.

'Back down with you - can't have you making the place look untidy.'

'Yes, sir,' Jack said quietly, his shoulders dropping. It seemed like he was fated to be stuck in the kitchen forever.

Retracing his steps, Jack climbed slowly back down again. He would either need a change of outfit or some other luck to be able to slip back to the upper deck and find Emmie. Emerging from the stairs, Jack heard raised voices and turned to see two men from the kitchen having a loud argument outside the door to the dining room. They were both really cross, and when one of them spotted him staring, he raised a fist and shook it menacingly in Jack's direction.

Quickly returning to the kitchen, Jack noticed that Bob was no longer at the sink and instead was being scolded in the corner of the room by an angry looking man in a dark uniform. Jack put his sack of flour down and tried to resume the pile of washing up as if nothing had happened, but it was never going to be that easy.

'He's back,' the boy said, pointing in Jack's direction. He looked over his shoulder and saw the angry looking man striding towards him, a few of the kitchen workers shrinking back as he passed. Jack gulped and wondered what was going to happen to him. He flinched as he saw the man begin to open his mouth but, instead of words, there was suddenly a loud ringing noise and the man stopped in his tracks.

The Search - Part 1

Emmie stood staring at the door for a few moments. She wasn't sure whether to be angry or relieved that there hadn't been a confrontation. As her and Jack thought they had realised last time, you have to be very careful not to change events in the past in case they have a different impact on the future.

Mary broke her stare by asking quietly - 'Do you think the boys might be in there?'

'I doubt it,' replied Emmie, turning to look at the girl - 'even if they were, I don't suppose they still will be. That man was really cross.' She was disappointed not to have been able to spot Jack - the ship was huge, and she had no way of knowing how many kitchens there might be - let alone where they all were. On their last adventure, she had Jack by her side - even if it was her looking after him most of the time. She felt really unsettled being somewhere unfamiliar on her own, even before the fact that they were currently trapped on a doomed ship.

Mary sniffed and wiped a tear away from her face - 'What if we don't find them before we get to America?' She looked down at the floor, and Emmie reached out to put an arm around her shoulder.

'Don't worry - it's not like they can get off,' reassured Emmie, forcing a smile, despite the knowledge that they had less time left than Mary thought.

There was a raised voice from the other side of the kitchen door, shortly joined by a second - it sounded like two people were having an argument. Mary tensed, her face looking uncomfortable.

'Why don't you go back and see if your dad has had any more luck finding them? I'll carry on looking upstairs.' She felt a bit guilty as she spoke - the real reason she wanted Mary to go back was so that she could focus on looking for Jack.

'Would you? Really? That's so kind,' replied Mary, immediately making Emmie feel even worse inside. The girl looked very relieved to be getting away from the angry voices still coming from the kitchen.

Resolving to keep an eye out for Patrick and John whilst she was searching for Jack, Emmie gave the smaller girl a grin. 'Why don't I meet you later and let you know what I've found out?' she suggested. 'How about in the dining room before bed?'

Mary nodded and skipped happily away. Emmie watched her disappear and deliberated her next move.

*

Walking quietly back across the room to the door which she knew led to the kitchen, Emmie pressed her ear to it and listened. There were footsteps moving around on the other side of the door now, and the argument seemed to have subsided.

Frowning to herself, Emmie wondered if she could go around and somehow access the kitchen from the other side. She wanted to find Jack as soon as possible, rather than wait and hope that he would find her. She turned and headed away from the kitchen door, hoping that she didn't bump into anyone who might wonder why she was alone in an empty dining room.

Descending to E deck, she turned right at the bottom of the staircase and followed the passageway forwards. There were lots of storerooms down here and plenty of people walking about - many carrying supplies, and with a purposeful air about them. No-one really paid her a second glance - she seemed to be smart enough to blend in with at least the 2nd class passengers, yet not overdressed for walking around the service areas of the ship.

As she carried on walking, Emmie noticed the hum of the engines getting louder as she passed the metal wall which she felt must be part of the engine room. She reached out a hand to touch the smooth surface and was sure she could feel some warmth coming through. Just over halfway along the arrow-straight passage, Emmie saw a narrow door, with a glazed porthole in the middle. She stopped and peered through the glass, noticing that there was a staircase on the other side. Glancing behind her, she pulled the door open and slipped through, stepping onto a much plusher carpet than she was expecting. The metal walls of E deck had given way to wooden panelling once more, and the doorway facing her was significantly wider than the one she had just passed through.

As Emmie stood there, a well-dressed lady emerged from the door opposite and started up the staircase. She was wearing a long, flowing dress and carrying a small bag. Just as she reached the first landing, a small man dressed in a dinner suit came hurrying out of the door after her. 'Hold on, dear,' he called out, slightly red in the face.

Emmie was sure she caught a rather rude reply from further up the stairs and sniggered to herself quietly. However, it seemed her definition of quietly wasn't quite the same as the red-faced man, and he turned to glare at her as he ascended.

Curious as to how the richer passengers on Titanic might live, Emmie walked over to the large door and pulled it open for a quick look. This side of the ship was totally different to the one she had just walked down - it looked like a posh hotel, with doors to bedrooms - or cabins in this case - set at regular intervals as far as she could see. These must be 1st class cabins as the distance between the doors suggested they were much bigger than the ones she had seen elsewhere on the ship.

A number of people were coming out of their cabins along the corridor - everyone seemed to be very dressed up and she wondered if they were heading out to some kind of evening entertainment. Feeling out of place, Emmie turned and stepped back through the door into the stairwell. She looked upwards and then headed for D deck above. Climbing one flight of stairs and hoping to emerge on the other side of the kitchen, she found herself in a reception room set out with round tables and heavy wicker chairs, where a few people sat chatting. The ceiling was ornately decorated with plasterwork and all the wood was painted white. At the end were big sets of double doors either side. She walked casually over to the doors and gently pushed one open a crack.

She could see a vast dining room beyond - set out with heavy white tablecloths and candlesticks in the centre of each table. There were a few boys, not much older than her by the look of them, arranging some cutlery on the furthest tables. One looked up at her and half smiled, before carrying on with his task.

'You're a bit late for supper, miss!' Emmie jumped and turned around - at one of the tables an older man was just getting up from where he had been sitting.

'Uh, I forgot something earlier,' Emmie muttered in his direction, 'can't see it though.' She forced a smile at the man as he passed her, before turning and slowly walking back across the room. She was sure he was trying to be friendly but didn't want to draw his attention to her either.

Finding herself back by the stairs, Emmie could see that one side of the reception area was definitely quieter than the other, and slowly walked around the edge of the room, making a pretence of looking out of the large, arch-topped windows.

As she walked, Emmie kept glancing subtly over her shoulder to work out the point where she wouldn't be observed as the central wall would hide her. Once she was confident that she had passed out of sight of any of the seated passengers, she quickened her pace and headed for the second set of double doors.

Pushing one of these doors open a crack, she looked in the direction of where the boys had been laying tables a few moments earlier. To her relief, they appeared to have gone and she slipped quietly through the door, letting it close against her hand to avoid making any noise. Feeling pretty sure that this must be the 1st class dining room, and likely the other side of the kitchens she had been searching for, Emmie felt her heart rate quicken. Jack could be just the other side of this room - the problem was, how was she going to find him without being observed?

Walking as silently as she could across the vast room, Emmie struggled to take in the opulence of it all. Each table was now laid for the next morning's breakfast - china and several sets of cutlery in every place setting. The chairs were all ornately carved in dark wood and set close to their tables - ready to be pulled out by the next occupants.

Reaching the nearest set of doors, Emmie stopped and tried to think rationally - she couldn't just stroll on into the kitchen as she would stand out immediately. She strained to listen through the door but couldn't hear anything this time. Noticing a keyhole near the handle, she bent down and put her eye to it - it was hard to see anything useful as the field of view was so narrow, but she thought the room looked dark.

Emmie stood back up, arguing internally with herself - should she just open the door and see if Jack was there? What if someone else was in the room? Deciding she really didn't have much to lose by looking, she gently placed a palm on the door and pressed it open a crack.

Heart beating wildly, Emmie snuck a look through the gap in the door and managed to confirm that it was the kitchen, and it was in semi-darkness. Opening the door more fully, she could see long, marble-topped work surfaces and rows and rows of cupboards. Racks of utensils hung from the ceiling and most of the walls too. There were no windows in this space, just a couple of ventilation grilles, which was causing the gloomy ambience. Some light was filtering through doors at the end of the room and Emmie wondered where they led. This kitchen was quite small compared to the enormity of the dining room which it presumably served - maybe there was a further one beyond it?

Emmie crept across the kitchen, trying to avoid her steps ringing out on the metal floor. As she reached the doors at the end, she froze - sure that there had been a rustling noise coming from the other side. These doors were not fully shut - helping with the light, but also making it more difficult to approach discreetly. Listening hard, Emmie wondered whether she might have imagined the noise as it didn't seem to recur.

Suddenly, the clang of footsteps rang out - making Emmie jump in shock. Someone was walking through the adjacent room, and they were heading right for the door.

The Smoking Room

'All hands to dessert stations!' announced the uniformed man in a grand voice, seemingly forgetting that he had been about to vent his anger on Jack. As he turned gratefully to follow his fellow kitchen workers through the doors and into the adjacent pastry kitchen, Jack felt sure he could feel the man's eyes boring into his back. He made a mental note to try and avoid any run-ins with him in the future, though the man seemed to be in a position of authority in the kitchens.

As he stepped through into the pastry kitchen, Jack could see plates of eclairs and dishes of ice cream laid out in neat rows. As he watched, each kitchen hand in front of him took one of each and carried it through the double doors into the dining room.

The grand space was no less impressive than when he had first seen it earlier. On this occasion, he tried to take in the room as he handed out desserts to the 1st class diners, following the lead of those in front of him. 'Ice cream, madam?' he asked as he approached the next table, handing over the dish when an affirmative answer was received.

As he made his way back to the kitchen for more food, Jack noticed a man with a thick white beard sitting at a table in the centre of the dining room. He had a number of other passengers at his table, and they were all talking animatedly. 'That's the captain,' a boy at his side whispered as they crossed the patterned tiles of the floor together.

'Here, boy - can you fetch me a cigar?' asked an elderly American man, as Jack placed his latest plate of eclairs down on a table.

'Yes... Certainly, sir,' Jack replied after a momentary hesitation. Where on earth was he going to find a cigar? He walked quickly back towards the kitchen and noticed the boy who had told him about the captain was coming the other way.

'Hey - where would I get a cigar from?' Jack asked quietly. 'A man at the table I served asked for one.'

'You'll have to go up to the bar in the smoking room,' the boy replied. 'There's a spiral staircase which goes all the way up - it's in the other kitchen. Make sure you tell Mr Barrow first - he'll be after you otherwise.'

Jack smiled his thanks and headed back through the double doors - making for the staircase. As he passed the angry man from earlier, who he now realised was Mr Barrow, he quickly explained where he was going and received a nod of assent. Jack was going against the flow of everyone else now - dodging men and boys carrying plates and dishes and trying not to knock into anyone. He had a couple of narrow escapes where he swerved away just in time and managed to get through into the main kitchen unscathed.

Spotting the spiral stairs in the centre of the room, tucked up against a bulkhead, Jack headed over to them and began to climb - looking up as he went to ensure he wasn't going to collide with anyone coming down. The stairs wound their way up and up - much further than he was expecting.

After what seemed like an age and made him feel like a hamster climbing a corkscrew, Jack's nose told him that he'd arrived at the right deck for the smoking room. Emerging in a small compartment and exiting adjacent to the male toilets, he was suddenly in a heavily decorated room with a strong odour of tobacco smoke, despite the room being empty of passengers as it was mealtime.

As he walked across the room to the bar on the far side, his nose wrinkled at the smell, and he tried not to sneeze. What struck him most about this space were the intricate stained-glass panels set in the walls. They were backlit and reminded him more of a church than a recreational space onboard a ship.

'Can I have a cigar please?' Jack said, as he approached the bar.

'Not for you, is it?' came the reply from the dinner suited barman. His hair was slicked back, and a neat moustache sat in the centre of his top lip.

'Err, no...' started Jack. 'It's for one of the passengers at dinner.'

'Just kidding you,' the barman handed over a carved wooden box and invited Jack to select a cigar. Luckily, they all looked the same, as he knew nothing about cigars, so he took the topmost one and smiled his thanks.

As Jack walked back across the blue and red tiles of the smoking room floor, he saw the first passengers returning from dinner, back to their favourite haunt and quickened his pace - eager to be out of the room before it filled with smoke again. He slipped back through the door next to the toilets and began to go down the spiral stairs. Almost immediately, he became aware of footsteps below him, and they sounded like their owner was coming upwards.

Reaching an exit part way down, Jack stepped out of the stairwell for a moment to allow the person coming up to pass by, and found himself in another kitchen, albeit smaller than the one he had just left. As the footsteps grew louder and the body they belonged to appeared, Jack was disappointed to see that it was Mr Barrow. He took a further step back involuntarily and hoped the man would pass by without noticing him. It wasn't to be, however, and the man stepped into the kitchen, his face clouding as he saw Jack again.

'What are you doing up here, boy?' he asked with an annoyed tone. 'How many times do I have to tell you?'

'Sorry sir,' replied Jack, though he really wanted to say something less polite. 'I was asked to come up and get a cigar for one of the passengers. I did ask you before I came up.' He reached into his pocket and held the cigar aloft, as if to demonstrate his point.

The man grunted - 'Well you'd better not keep him waiting then,' before disappearing through a door. As it swung gently closed behind him, Jack caught a burble of conversation and could see a restaurant space beyond. Slowly descending the spiral staircase once more, he thought about the route he had been taken on to the kitchen when they first arrived - they had definitely walked past a restaurant, and he was fairly sure it was on this deck. Maybe once the dinner service was over and Mr Barrow let him leave, he could use these stairs to sneak back up and search for Emmie?

Pleased with his deduction, he finished walking down the steps and back through the kitchen, still carefully carrying the cigar. The pastry kitchen was much quieter now - most of the desserts having been carried out and replaced with dishes needing washing up. Jack shuddered to himself - he hated doing the dishes, but it looked like there was a lot of work still to do this evening.

He pushed the door into the dining room open and looked around for the man who had asked for the cigar. It had only been ten minutes or so previously, but Jack couldn't recall what he looked like. He decided to hold the cigar and walk slowly around, in the hope that the man would see and beckon him over. There were a lot less people in the dining room than there had been earlier - a number of guests having departed for various evening entertainments.

On this occasion though, Jack's luck was in - at the third table he passed, a man turned to him and reached out for the cigar. 'Thank you,' he said to Jack, before pressing a silver coin into his hand and turning back to the table.

Jack walked away, looking down at the coin as he did so. He turned it over in his hand - one side said 'United States of America' and the other 'One Dime'. He had no idea what a dime was, or how much it was worth, but it would be a nice memento of their adventure. He had kept a shiny penny from their trip to 1940, and it was one of his most treasured possessions. Slipping the coin into his pocket, he resolved to show Emmie later when they met up.

He pushed the door open into the pastry kitchen, seeing that there were plates of hot food laid out now and some of the kitchen staff were tucking in. This was obviously how they ate their meals to fit around those who they cooked for and waited on. Jack took a plate and tucked in hungrily - there was boiled meat and potatoes, with plenty of gravy - after his exertions during the evening he was certainly hungry.

*

When he got back into the main kitchen, Jack saw that Mr Barrow was back. He was directing the enormous washing up operation - plates, glasses and serving dishes were all being carried to the long row of sinks, then washed and dried, before being stacked in special cupboards just outside the kitchen. Jack disliked chores a lot and would always try to avoid tidying his bedroom or helping around the house at home. He was pleased to have earned some money for fetching the cigar and this made him feel a bit more positive about the enforced clearing up duties. Trying his best to get a 'putting away' job, Jack stood at the end of the drying line, but the man saw him and nudged him in the direction of the stacked, dirty plates instead.

Resigning himself to this fate, Jack began carrying handfuls of crockery over to the sinks to be washed. He marvelled at the amount of waste from these 1st class passengers - some were sending back whole plates of food, barely touched. One boy seemed to have a full-time job scraping the mountains of food waste into a bin in the corner of the kitchen, which was occasionally closed and gave off a hissing sound, before being opened and re-filled.

Spinning the sink tap to turn it on, Jack looked around for a cloth, then jumped as a clang, followed by a whooshing sound, came from the sink. He turned back to see a fountain of water arcing upwards from the tap and the wheel he had spun lying useless in the bottom of the sink. Thinking quickly, he tried to press his hand over the spurting water, but only succeeded in squirting it over the boy next to him. The boy shouted for Mr Barrow, who came running across the kitchen, looking as disapproving as ever, and fumbled with the separated tap. He managed to put it back together again, but not before getting a good drenching himself.

'What are you playing at?' he snarled at Jack, directing him to the other end of the workstation and the pile of plates waiting to be put away. Jack breathed a small sigh of relief as the man walked off to get dry, leaving him to play his part in the human chain stacking everything in the right cupboards. Relieved to finally hear that all kitchen hands were now off duty until breakfast started, he wondered about finding Emmie.

Looking around and watching the majority of the workers leave through the doors at the end of the kitchen, heading for the stairs down to E deck and their beds, Jack waited until the room was a little quieter and then edged his way over to the spiral staircase. Quickly checking that no-one was paying him any attention, he stepped onto the stairs and began to climb. Up and up he went, starting to feel the reality of their situation kicking in, now he was free to try and do something about it again.

Reaching the exit on the restaurant level, Jack carefully ducked his head into the kitchen and was relieved to see that it was deserted and in partial darkness - a sliver of light from under the door providing the only illumination. Tiptoeing over to the door, Jack cracked it open and peered through - despite the lights being on, it didn't seem that there was anyone present. Walking swiftly through the empty restaurant, Jack suddenly froze as he heard coughing coming from an office near the main exit.

He paused for several long seconds, wondering whether to go back or carry on - deciding in the end that the person coughing didn't seem to be coming out. Quietly making his exit, Jack passed a long line of coat and hat hooks on the wall, before emerging into the reception space he had entered with Emmie earlier that day. It was quite empty, so he made his way over to one of the tables and sat down to wait.

The Search - Part 2

The door opened and Emmie stepped back, staring in surprise at the man facing her. She saw that he held some bread in his hand and his eyes were wide with shock. He had obviously not expected anyone to still be in this part of the ship after dinner had finished either.

Another half second passed, and then the man turned on his heels and ran back through the kitchen, his footsteps echoing in the silent room. Emmie's mind raced - what was he doing in here? Could he be up to no good - or was he just hungry?

'Hey!' she called out on impulse after the receding figure, 'have you seen a boy with orange hair?' Listening hard, Emmie thought that the footsteps slowed for a moment as the man heard her shout, but then a door banged further inside the kitchen. Emmie walked quickly through the now-deserted room, heading for the door, which was still swinging gently.

Placing a palm on the door, Emmie steadied the motion and then gently eased it open. There was no sign of anyone in the passage beyond, as she opened the door wider and slipped through the gap. Listening again, she walked hesitantly forward, peering in the first open doorway which appeared on her right. It seemed to be some sort of storage cupboard - shelves of plates lined every wall, all neatly stacked in size order. The next room held glassware and the following one, china - all organised and ready for the next service. Feeling emboldened, Emmie continued along the passage and reached the door at the end. She passed through it, immediately noticing a number of voices coming from around the corner, past a stairwell.

Pressing herself against the wall, Emmie edged towards the corner, risking a quick look around the dull, grey metal wall. At first, she couldn't see anyone, but then realised there were a couple of men carrying sacks up and down a small set of stairs at the far side of the ship. She wondered whether or not she would be able to make the main stairwell without being spotted. It was probably only ten seconds of quick walking, but she would have to time it really well.

Waiting for exactly the right moment, Emmie stepped confidently out in the passage and headed for the stairs. Just as she was about to ascend, there was a clatter of footsteps and two loud, male voices carried down from the deck above.

Shocked, but reacting quickly, Emmie turned on her heels and quickly retraced her steps - just making it back around the corner before the owners of the voices stepped into the passage. She quietly opened the door and stole through it, but not before she heard a fragment of the newcomers' conversation.

'Davis said there was a kid down here earlier,' the first voice announced. The reply was muffled, but Emmie was fairly sure that she heard the words 'find them' as the door swung shut behind her.

Not waiting to find out if the men were heading in the same direction as her, Emmie moved back towards the kitchen as fast as she could manage. She looked around - trying to gauge if there were any good hiding places. All of the cupboards were too small to fit in, and what looked like a storeroom at the end turned out to be a coal bunker. She could hide in there, but it was filthy, and ruining her clothes wouldn't help in the search for Jack.

Valuable seconds ticked by, and Emmie could feel the blood pounding through her veins - she knew that at any moment the men searching this deck could open the various doors into the kitchen and find her in there. She was about to head back into the dining room when she spotted a small spiral staircase tucked away behind one of the central bulkheads. Heading over to it, she started to climb the steps just in time - hearing the searchers enter the kitchen below her.

The staircase wound up through the ship and Emmie felt like it was never going to end - she held her breath for at least two decks in height before the first opportunity to get off presented itself. She emerged into another kitchen, smaller this time, which appeared to lead onto yet another dining area. The door between them had a circle of frosted glass with a clear ring around it - cleverly allowing a discreet view out into the dining room from the kitchen. Emmie squinted through the glass and could see the room was empty.

Walking quickly through it, she found herself on a long corridor which led onto a reception room with a grand staircase in the centre. Allowing herself a small smile of triumph, Emmie realised that this was the very space that they had emerged into from the tunnel. It made sense now why the room had been so busy, and then deserted - it must be used as a waiting area for the restaurant, and they had come out just as the doors were opening for dinner.

Emmie wondered if Jack was going to find his way back - she'd told him to try and meet at the staircase and wasn't having much luck finding him. Two heads would be much better than one in trying to work out how to get home, now the tunnel appeared blocked. The room was quiet, although there was some music drifting from the grand staircase - it was hard to tell if it was coming from above or below though. Emmie's eyes wandered to the door they'd arrived through - it was still partially obscured with the heavy curtain and looked to be shut.

Walking over to the door and turning the handle, Emmie paused. What if she somehow stepped back into the present without Jack? Without understanding exactly how all of this worked, there felt like a real risk of that happening if she went in alone. Would he be able to find his way back without her? She snatched her hand away from the door as if it had been burned - there would be no opening it until they were both safely there. Just in case...

Feeling a little unsure what to do next, Emmie wandered across the reception room, staring at the huge staircase in the centre. It was definitely a statement - designed to look both imposing and to show off the skills of the craftspeople who had carved it. She suddenly felt very lonely and thought about investigating where the music was coming from. Now she was level with the staircase, she was fairly sure that it was drifting from one of the decks above. It was quite faint still and sounded like a piano.

In the end, her curiosity won out and Emmie carefully climbed the staircase. She was pleased with herself for not meeting anyone on the way up but, as she turned at the top, a crowd of men emerged from what smelled like a smoking room and passed her, chatting animatedly. Thinking that they hadn't noticed her, Emmie almost jumped when the last man said 'Hello, miss,' and smiled at her. Emmie managed a smile back, and then breathed a sigh of relief when they had gone - she obviously didn't look too out of place up here after all.

The aroma of stale smoke, and close run-in with her fellow passengers, gave Emmie a sudden urge for some fresh air and she walked across to the large, glazed doors which led out onto the promenade deck. It was dark outside now and, as soon as she stepped through the doors, she partially regretted her decision. An April night in the mid-Atlantic was by no means warm, and it felt like the prevailing wind was blowing down the length of the promenade, enveloping her with icy fingers.

Shivering to herself, Emmie pulled the jacket tighter around her shoulders and took in several deep lungfuls of the chilled air. The hit of oxygen to her brain helped her think more clearly - she'd told Jack to meet her back by the stairs and that's what he would inevitably do. She'd managed to find her way there, so there wasn't any reason that he wouldn't either. Was there?

Despite the cold, Emmie didn't feel ready to go back inside the ship yet, so she walked along the deck for a few moments. There were deckchairs carefully stacked by the side furthest from the rail and, as she walked, she was able to peer into the smoking room through some small windows. Through the swirling clouds of tobacco smoke, she noticed that the room was laid out much like the other 1st class areas of the ship - heavy wooden furniture and ornate panelling. It appeared to be lit with electric lamps, as they weren't flickering like candles or gas lamps would.

Deciding that it was definitely too cold out here for walking any further, Emmie turned to the rail at the edge of the deck. She paused for a moment, staring out into the inky blackness, with just the smallest slivers of moonlight dancing across the wavetops. The sea sounded a long way beneath her as she stood near the top of this giant ship, and it made her feel far from home.

Turning on her heels, Emmie strode quickly back along the deck - now seeking warmth rather than fresh air. As she reached for the door handle to go back inside, she noticed a figure in a dark coat, partially hidden by a bulwark. She stared for half a moment too long, and the person seemed to sense her presence and looked up.

'If you are searching for something, you should probably look where you least expect to find it,' said the figure, cryptically. Emmie jumped - not expecting to be spoken to, and certainly not in such an unusual way. Her grip tightened on the door handle as her impulse was to get away, but something stopped her. Looking more closely at the figure, she could see that it was an older man with a kindly face. She paused and looked quizzically at the man, who briefly wished her good luck before turning and walking away. Emmie stared after him - what was that about? Had he mistaken her for someone else?

As she stepped back inside the ship, rubbing the warmth back into her arms, Emmie walked back to the top of the steps and looked down into the reception room once more. Sat at one of the tables facing the stairs, was a tall boy with orange hair. He was looking nervously back and forth between the door and the stairs, and she could see him tapping his foot against the table leg.

'Jack!' she called, waving frantically as he looked up at her and grinned. She clattered down the steps, two at a time, and ran to him. Hugging Jack close to her, Emmie felt the worry of the past few hours drain away - he was alright and, more importantly, they were back together.

Back Together

Stepping back a bit, Emmie looked at Jack curiously. 'Why are you wearing that jacket?' she asked, 'what have you been up to?'

Jack looked down at himself - he'd remembered to take the apron off but had obviously forgotten the jacket. His own school blazer was still hanging up down in the kitchen too. He looked at Emmie and answered - 'It turned out that school uniform didn't quite fit in with the kitchen crew...'

Emmie half smiled - 'What happened then?' The smile disappeared again as she remembered him being marched away. 'I was really scared when that man took you off. Worried for where you might be going, but more worried because we're going to have to figure out how to get home, and two heads are definitely better than one.'

'He took me to the kitchen. Seemed to think I was someone else and that I'd sneaked away and was skiving,' Jack explained, his face indignant at this point. 'He kept calling me Baxter... I don't know who the man was, but he seemed to be in charge of the kitchens in some way.'

'How did you manage to get away?' Emmie was intrigued - it had seemed like Jack was a virtual prisoner when he walked off earlier.

'Well, I tried a few times, but people kept stopping me and sending me back to work. It's not been a picnic - that's for sure.' Jack's eyes lit up - 'I tell you what though - this ship is enormous! I've not seen half of it, but you could walk for miles and not go down the same corridor twice. There's even a spiral staircase right through the middle of the ship from the kitchens up to the top!'

Emmie nodded - 'I know, I found that too.'

Jack's eyes bulged a bit at this point - 'How did you get into the kitchen? I didn't see you...'

'Well, I've spent most of the time since you disappeared looking for you, actually,' came the retort. Emmie didn't want to admit exactly how terrified at being alone she had felt, but she couldn't have him thinking she wasn't bothered either. 'I think I must have come into the kitchen after you finished because it was all quiet - well, except for a man who seemed to be stealing food.'

'Really?' asked Jack, 'what happened then?'

'Oh, he ran off when I opened the door and saw him - I'm not sure who was more surprised actually! Then a couple of the crew came in searching for some missing boys - I had to look for somewhere to hide, and that's when I found the spiral staircase.'

'Missing boys?'

'Yeah - I heard them talking and thought I'd better get out of there quickly. I think they might have been looking for Patrick and John.'

'Patrick and John? Who are they?' In one breath, Emmie had said she'd been looking for him, but now she was making new friends?

It all came tumbling out then - how Emmie had wandered around the ship, searching for him on different decks and eventually found Mary crying in the corridor. 'So, I was looking for you and trying to find them at the same time,' she finished.

'And you think they were playing in the lift, which is when Mary thought they'd vanished?' confirmed Jack. He chuckled - 'Imagine thinking a lift was magic!'

Emmie smiled - 'You've got to remember she's from a small village in Ireland over 100 years ago - she'd probably never seen a ship before Titanic either...'

'So, what's the plan then?' asked Jack. 'How do we get out of here with the tunnel blocked? Any great ideas, as I'd really like to go home?' He looked across at the door they'd originally entered through and stood up abruptly - 'Let's start by finding out if it is still blocked?'

As he took the first couple of steps towards the door, two ladies swept down the stairs in front of them and staggered, giggling slightly, over to a sofa right next to the door. They sat down heavily and started an animated conversation. Emmie stood, reaching out for Jack's arm, and steered him past the door and round the corner back towards the restaurant.

'Hmmph,' sighed Jack, 'that's typical.' His face was downcast, and he felt close to tears. How on earth did you get off a ship stuck in the past when your only known exit was blocked...? 'I want to go now.' Jack's voice raised in pitch a little - 'It was April 13th when this started and, assuming it's the same date here, we've got a little over a day - Titanic sank in the early hours of April 15th.'

There was a pause - it only lasted a few seconds but felt like an eternity. Neither of them spoke, both just staring at each other - the scarcity of time hitting them like a train. The pair knew how this would end for the ship and that, without a way out, they would be in a lot of danger, but the realisation of just how little time was left felt overwhelming.

Searching for something constructive to say, Emmie suddenly remembered the strange man she had seen out on the deck. 'I met someone earlier,' she told Jack, explaining about the brief conversation outside. 'He seemed to know that I was looking for something and said I should look where I was least expecting to find it.'

'What does that mean?' sniffed Jack. 'The way out of here...?'

Emmie's brow furrowed in concentration - 'Maybe... Though he could have been referring to Mary's lost brothers too.'

'Or he could have been crazy,' Jack added rudely. 'It's a bit tenuous, isn't it?'

'We haven't got a lot else at the moment, have we?' Emmie reached out to put her arm around Jack - they needed to stay positive if they were going to figure out a way back. 'It's late,' she said, 'tell you what, why don't we find somewhere to sleep and get searching for an exit in the morning? It'll be easier when we're not tired.'

Jack nodded - 'You're right,' he said quietly, 'I think we need to stick together to stand the best chance though.'

'Ok - best stay out of the way of the kitchen staff then,' she joked in reply. 'I said I'd meet Mary before bed to tell her what I'd found - you should come too.'

Jack nodded and Emmie grinned encouragingly at him. 'Mary's downstairs on F deck - shall we go back down the spiral stairs?'

'Yep - let's go.'

Jack led the way back through the restaurant, pausing to check if there was anyone in the office this time. Everywhere was in darkness, so they crept into the small kitchen and slowly went down the steps. There was no-one about, but the constant hum of the engines masked any noise their feet may have made on the metal stairs. As they emerged into the kitchen, Jack headed for the coat hooks and retrieved his blazer - swapping it for the chef's jacket he had been wearing.

'At least you look less like you've just escaped now,' Emmie joked. Walking quietly, she led Jack through to the 2nd class dining room and the stairwell contained within it. They slipped down a level to E deck, and then Emmie breathed a sigh of relief - at least they wouldn't get into trouble for being down here.

Jack recognised parts of where he'd walked along earlier and showed Emmie some of the storerooms that he'd observed along the long, wide service passageway. Even though it was late, there was a lot of activity down here - passengers walking to and from their cabins, mixed in with ship workers fetching and carrying. It felt like this more utilitarian part of the ship never slept.

As they neared the end of the corridor, Emmie pointed out the door she'd slipped through earlier which led to the 1st class cabins. Jack pointed to a sign - 'Port use only - that means you weren't supposed to open it,' he said, with mock seriousness.

'Oh well,' replied Emmie, 'it was interesting seeing how the other half live. The cabins through there are huge compared to the ones on this side.'

Arriving at a narrow double staircase, Emmie indicated downwards - 'Only one more deck.' The battleship-grey metal continued unrelentingly down the stairs, and Jack noticed that it felt a degree or two colder as they descended.

'Where's her cabin?' Jack asked. Everything in this part of the ship looked the same - rows and rows of doors set almost alongside each other - so small were the cabins they belonged to.

'Oh!' Emmie replied, slapping her palm against her forehead in frustration. 'I said I'd meet her in the 3rd class dining room - I thought it was this way, but it's not...'

Jack grumbled at this setback, but followed Emmie back up the grey stairs. They retraced their steps until they saw a large double staircase with a small sign indicating the 3rd class dining room was below them. Clattering down the stairs in excitement, the pair emerged into a narrow area in the centre of the dining room.

The room was brightly lit - at odds with the rest of the dining areas they had been through. This one, however, wasn't empty - it seemed to be being used as a recreational space between meals. There were quite a few groups of people sitting around chatting - mainly women and some children.

Emmie and Jack slowly walked around the room - Emmie's eyes scanning for Mary in amongst the other occupants. They completed a circuit without seeing the smaller girl and arrived back at the bottom of the stairs.

'What now?' Jack asked. 'Maybe her brothers came back already?'

'My brothers?' came a soft Irish voice from behind them, 'did you find them?'

Jack jumped, and Emmie turned around with a smile on her face. 'Mary - we couldn't see you - where were you?'

'I just went to get a glass of water,' the girl replied, indicating a door behind her. 'So - did you find John and Patrick?'

'No, I'm afraid not,' explained Emmie, recounting the various places which she'd searched in. Mary wasn't to know that the main object of her search so far had been Jack.

Mary's hopeful expression faded, and she looked at her feet. 'Father is going to be so angry when they do show up,' she admitted, 'I'd really like to find them first.'

'They can't have gone far,' suggested Jack - 'there's nowhere to go.'

'Oh, Mary - this is Jack,' Emmie explained. The girl looked a bit confused, so Emmie went on quickly - 'he's got a job in the kitchens, and I thought he could help me look.'

'Tell you what,' Jack offered, 'why don't we all go looking together tomorrow morning? We probably stand a better chance if there's more of us to hunt.'

'Oh, yes please,' agreed Mary, her face lighting up, 'we can start at the bottom again, and go as far up as we can.'

'Put your best frock on and I think we could just about get away with going everywhere,' suggested Emmie. 'If we look confident, then we should be able to do it. Let's meet back down here when you've had breakfast?'

Mary nodded, thinking it was slightly odd that Emmie was worried about her appearance but seemed to always wear the same clothes herself. 'See you in the morning,' she said.

As Mary headed back to her cabin, Jack leaned over to Emmie and spoke quietly - 'Where are we going to sleep tonight?'

Bad Dream

'We're going to have to split up for a bit,' said Emmie.

Jack looked at her quizzically - 'What do you mean?'

'I don't think we're going to find anywhere we can both sleep without people asking questions about where our parents are. You'd be better off looking for a cabin with the kitchen workers where there's a spare bunk.'

'Oh...' replied Jack. He wasn't really keen on them separating so quickly when it had been quite difficult to get back to Emmie in the first place. Besides, he didn't really want to run into the man from the kitchen again either. 'What about the tunnel? Can't we sleep in there - it's not like anyone is going to come in and disturb us?'

'The cold, damp tunnel you mean? The one with a stone floor...? I'm not keen on splitting up either, but that doesn't sound like a nice place to sleep.'

'What will you do?' Jack asked.

'I'm going to see if I can find a spare bunk in the section near Mary's family. Hopefully I can blend in down here.'

'Why don't you see if you can sleep in Mary's cabin?' Jack wanted to know where Emmie was going to be - he felt less alone that way.

'She said her dad was quite strict,' Emmie explained, 'I don't suppose he'd like someone turning up in their cabin unexpectedly.' Putting an arm around Jack, she squeezed his shoulder - 'Meet you for breakfast?'

He half-grinned - 'Sure, sounds like a plan. I'll be giving the kitchen a wide berth in the morning though!'

'Ok - let's meet here then? We can see if Patrick and John have turned up. If not, then we can help Mary look for them - gives us a chance to see more of Titanic, and hopefully figure out a way home.'

Jack nodded - 'Alright then. Night...'

'Night, Jack.'

*

As he walked up the stairs on the only route out of the dining room and found himself in the wide corridor of

E deck, Jack realised that this was where the staff cabins were located. He was a bit reluctant to start trying doors as he wasn't sure what he might find behind them. Instead, he wandered slowly down the corridor, trying to figure out which cabin might have a spare bunk. He could hear loud snoring coming from behind a number of the doors, and this didn't inspire him to venture within.

He came to a door which obviously led to a toilet or bathroom and went inside. Deciding to use one of the cubicles whilst he was there, he sat down just as a couple of men came in, talking quietly. Overhearing their conversation, Jack discovered that one of the waiters cabins a few doors further back along the corridor seemed to have some empty bunks in. Waiting until the men had departed, Jack left the cubicle, washed his hands, and went back into the corridor.

The first door he tried opened out into a large, dimly lit room. He could make out bunks all around the edge of the space, and also in rows down the middle of the room. As he stood in the doorway, trying to see if any beds were vacant, there came an angry shout from further inside the room - 'Close that blooming door!'

Spooked, Jack quickly stepped back outside the cabin and shut the door. Breathing heavily, he leaned against the cool steel wall of the corridor and debated what to do next. He almost started walking towards the rear of the boat, where Emmie had intended to find a berth, but then pulled himself together and moved towards the next cabin door along.

It was ajar - light obviously filtering in from the corridor without annoying the occupants - so he decided to try his luck once more. He gently pushed the door open and stepped inside. Instead of standing surveying the room, he walked slowly but confidently across to the far corner - pleased to see there were three empty bunks alongside some lockers.

Jack sat down on the lower of the bunks, figuring that he would make less noise if he avoided climbing any ladders. As his eyes accustomed to the gloom, he could see the shapes of sleeping people in most of the other beds. It was fairly quiet in the cabin, save for some snoring and the ever-present thrum of the engines, which vibrated throughout the metal-clad parts of the ship.

The bed had a mattress and pillow on it, and there appeared to be clean blankets folded up at the foot. Jack's luck was in - it didn't look like this bunk had been slept in at all yet. He quietly slipped off his shoes, shrugged the blazer from his shoulders and unfolded the blanket. As he curled up underneath it, he reflected on the most unbelievable of days so far. After London in the Blitz, he never thought he would get the chance to step through time again - but here he was, surging across the Atlantic, en-route to New York in a ship which would never get there...

Eventually, tiredness won out and Jack's eyelids began to droop. As he fell asleep, he dreamed he was back in the air raid shelter with Emmie, the roar of bombers flying overhead, and the rhythmic thump of explosions. One particularly close blast shook him awake and he sat up, sweat dripping from his forehead and uncertain where he was.

The room was still in virtual darkness, but there was a loud, monotonous hum coming from outside in the corridor. He half stood up, slightly unsure if he was still dreaming or not.

'Go back to sleep, lad. They're just running the engines up to full speed - often do it at night to avoid disturbing the passengers.' The voice belonged to a shadowy figure in the next bunk, who then put his pillow over his head in an attempt to block out further noise.

Jack sat down again, wiping his forehead with the back of his hand. The hum was a lot louder than when he had gone to sleep but, now he thought about it, the sound was quite similar. So much for not disturbing the passengers though - the noise was loud enough to wake the heaviest of sleepers. It then dawned on him that the metal walls in this part of the ship probably amplified the sound - there was no wooden panelling for the likes of them. Shuffling back under the blanket, Jack also put his pillow over his head and eventually returned to sleep.

*

The next morning, Jack was awoken by an alarm, buzzing insistently just outside the cabin. He opened one eye and saw the shapes in bunks around him become human as they stretched and sat up. The alarm was obviously to signal the crew to get up, as the men in the cabin began pulling on their clothes and shoes.

Jack looked around him - the floor of the room was covered in a pale pink linoleum, and the bunks had white painted metal frames. There was a bare light fitting in the centre of the room, and a stack of small lockers to the side of his bunk. The other occupants all seemed to be much older than him and he wondered where the younger boys from the kitchen might have slept. No-one really gave Jack a second glance as he too stretched, got up and started to pull on his shoes. Having slept in his clothes last night meant that Jack had less to do in order to get ready, but his shirt in particular was now very creased. Never mind, he thought, hoping that his jacket would obscure it.

The men in the cabin started to file outside and Jack wondered what to do - adamant that he didn't want to get stuck in the kitchen again. He decided to follow the workers and then find an opportunity to sneak away. Most of the men walked along the corridor and took a small set of stairs to the left. Jack could smell the aroma of baking bread wafting down to him and realised that this was the way to the kitchen. Taking a deep breath, he carried on past the stairs and focused on a point further down the corridor, despite the overwhelming urge to look back over his shoulder.

He had probably got about twenty paces past the stairs when there was a shout behind him - 'Oi - where are you going?!' Adrenaline kicked in and Jack ran down the corridor as fast as he could, dodging around crew members as he went. Up ahead, a door was slightly ajar, and he slowed enough to grab at the handle and wrench it open, before throwing himself inside.

Jack's momentum caused him to tumble onto the floor, and he landed on what seemed like a huge pile of laundry. Scrabbling upright and with his heart beating fast, he frantically looked around the room for a better hiding place - his eyes settling onto a small sliding door, set low into the back wall. He pulled it open and saw that it led to some kind of chute. Without really stopping to think, he swung his legs over the edge and dropped.

Suddenly, Jack was in darkness - the chute sloping steeply down and turning this way and that. If he wasn't so desperate to get away from whoever was chasing him, then this might actually be quite fun. The chute took a final hard twist to the left, and then Jack found himself sailing through the air and landing with a hard thump on the floor. He sat up, rubbing his hip which had taken most of the impact, and realised that this was likely a laundry room.

The room was in semi-darkness, with a small amount of light filtering through a grille in the door - which Jack hoped would be unlocked. He got stiffly to his feet and tried the door handle - thankfully it opened. Outside was a corridor, and he could see some steps to his left, which he cautiously ascended, finding himself back in the wide corridor where he had started from.

Jack's first impulse was to go back down the stairs again - he really didn't want to run into Mr Barrow or any of the other kitchen staff. The problem was that Emmie would be waiting for him in the 3rd class dining room, and that was back towards the kitchen too. He would have to be both alert and brave - well, braver than he felt right now at least.

Tucking in close to the wall of the corridor, Jack followed a man carrying a basket of fruit, until he reached the double staircase leading down to the dining room. He then peeled off and quickly walked down the steps, hoping that Emmie would already be there.

The Cleaner

Emmie woke early - there was only the merest hint of light creeping around the shuttered porthole window of the cramped cabin. She raised her head and looked slowly around - the cabin had four bunks, with a white basin set in between. The walls were panelled in a pale painted finish, and there was a faint smell of unwashed bodies. Laying back down on her pillow, Emmie tried to drop off again, but without success.

Last night, she had found herself back on F deck after a lengthy walk around the ship's lower levels. There were a lot of 3rd class cabins, but access to them was quite convoluted as they were at either end of the ship. At first, she had headed towards the front, following Jack, but a few moments behind him. It had become quickly obvious that this end of the ship was mainly for the crew and unaccompanied men, so she had retraced her steps.

Once rearward of the dining room, she had descended again and found herself in an area of 2nd class cabins. Not quite knowing the best way to seek out an empty bunk, she had tried several doors - only to find them locked. Feeling quite disheartened, she ventured still further back and went down the last set of stairs, just as the passageway curved to a stop at the ship's stern.

It was immediately obvious that these cabins were much smaller - several doors were ajar, which gave Emmie the confidence to peer inside. There were a couple of further false starts, and then Emmie chanced upon a cabin which appeared to only have two occupants - both snoring gently. She crept into the room and quietly curled up on one of the vacant bottom bunks, glad of the blanket laid out on top of the mattress. This deck was noisy with the rumbling note of the engines, and there was a constant vibration through the floor which continued up into her bunk. Covering her ears with each hand eventually allowed Emmie to fall into a fitful sleep.

She dreamed of lost boys running around and, at one point, was jolted awake by what she was convinced was the ship hitting an iceberg. Listening carefully to the noises outside the cabin, her mind was finally placated by the normality of what she could hear -

there was a change in engine note, but there were no signs of people moving around.

As she lay in the bunk trying to find sleep again, Emmie felt unsettled that she wasn't exactly sure of the current date. They had arrived in Belfast on April 13th, and it was logical that the date would be the same now, but could they guarantee it? She looked at the watch on her wrist, expecting to see that it was still stubbornly showing 24:00. It was, but as she stared at the glowing digits on the screen, it changed to 23:59. Rubbing her eyes, she looked again - it had definitely changed! What did it mean, and what had caused it to start working again?

Suddenly, a chill ran through her body - the watch must be counting down to when Titanic sank! If her guess around dates was correct, then it was now the early hours of April 14th - exactly twenty-four hours before the ship slipped below the waves forever...

*

Despite the earliness of the hour, Emmie decided to get up before the other occupants of the cabin awoke. She quietly rose and crossed the cabin floor to the door, reaching for the handle to ease it open. As she did so, a shaft of light from the corridor fell into the room and settled on one of the bunks opposite where she had been laying. The figure in the bunk twitched a little and then opened one eye.

'Oi! What's going on?!' came an angry hiss - at which point Emmie swiftly stepped across the threshold and shut the door. She quickly ran to the staircase and shot up it, covering three flights in record time. As she emerged outside the general room, she stopped - panting and with her heart beating fast. She pressed herself against the wall of the entrance space and tried to listen. Straining to hear, she thought there were footsteps ascending after her, but then silence. Feeling a little disorientated after having to react so quickly, Emmie decided to take a seat in the general room next door and wait for breakfast time.

The room was empty at this early hour - a low ceilinged space with fixed wooden benches running around the perimeter, and some tables and chairs in the centre. Emmie sat down on one of the benches, swinging her feet up and stretching out. She could see the sun beginning to rise out of the small windows - casting a milky glow around the room. Searching for a way home with Jack had taken on a new urgency now, as it had become clear that the ship would not see another dawn. Hopefully, they'd be able to help Mary find her brothers in the available time too. She stretched out a bit more - this bench was surprisingly comfortable.

*

'Are you ok, miss?' - someone was shaking Emmie's shoulder gently. She sat up with a start and realised that she must have fallen asleep on the bench.

'Err... Yes, thanks. I must have dropped off...' she replied - noticing that the man who had woken her was carrying a broom. 'Am I in your way?'

'No, miss - you're fine. I can sweep around you.' The man then sat down alongside Emmie, and she looked at him more closely - it was the strange man who had talked to her on the deck last night. She pushed herself away - alarmed at his presence and wondering what he wanted with her. The man smiled and spoke gently - 'I mean you no harm, but I have something very important to tell you.'

Emmie's eyes narrowed - he looked friendly, but she still felt suspicious of this stranger who seemed to be following her. The man continued - 'I asked you last night if you were searching for something. Were you looking for two missing boys?' The shock hit Emmie like a body blow - how did he know about Patrick and John? Was he involved in their disappearance?

Seeing her expression change, the man continued - 'I know you have travelled a long way to get here, and you're not sure of the route back.' At this, Emmie scrambled to her feet in fright - did the man know...? How could he? Her head whirling, Emmie tried to speak, but words didn't seem to be able to come out - instead she just stood ashen-faced, staring at the man.

'The thing is,' he said quietly, 'your previous adventure had quite an impact, and there's a small repair job to do.'

'W-what are you talking about? managed Emmie, 'what 'previous adventure'?'

'London in the Blitz.'

Those four words hung in the air for a very long time, as Emmie's legs turned to jelly, and she sat down heavily on the end of the bench. 'I know about it all,' said the man, 'and I'm here to help.'

Hardly believing she was having this conversation, Emmie whispered - 'What do you need us to do?'

The man stood, picking up his broom - 'Save Mary,' he said simply, before walking out of the room, leaving Emmie looking like she had seen a ghost.

Eventually pulling herself together, Emmie clattered down the stairs, heading for the dining room. It was breakfast time, but she wasn't hungry - the weight of the man's words sat like a knot in her stomach, and she needed to talk to Jack - quickly.

As she took the final steps down into the dining room, Emmie could see Jack sitting at a table with a large family alongside him. That was annoying - she would have to wait for them to go before she could talk to him properly. As she walked over to join him, she noticed that the room was very noisy, and the forward section, which she was sat in, seemed to be for family and female use - with the single men using the rear area. Emmie was still surprised by the level of segregation - it felt odd to separate men and women, as this was not something she was used to in modern life.

Jack saw her approaching and slid over a mug of tea. 'Sorry it's cold,' he explained, 'I've been here ages...' Emmie gave him a small smile - 'Thanks.' She took a sip of the lukewarm liquid and realised that the family seemed to be talking about the strange noise that had woken her during the night.

'I think they must have been running up the engines,' said the father to his wife. 'There was an awful racket at one point.'

'Are we going to get to America quicker?' asked one of the boys sat alongside.

'I don't know about that,' came the reply, 'but I wouldn't be surprised if they were trying to set some kind of speed record.'

'Wow - can we go out on the deck and watch later?'

'Why not,' the mother chimed in excitedly, 'I think it'll be great fun!'

Emmie breathed a sigh of relief - a small part of her still worried that the noise was an iceberg strike, and that no-one had realised yet. She knew the ship sank in the middle of the night but wasn't really sure how much earlier the damage was suffered. It sounded like the man had been awake for longer than her and been able to work out the source of the noise more accurately.

After what seemed like an eternity, the family got up and left. Emmie slid along the bench, closer to Jack. 'Are you ok?' he asked, 'you're very quiet, and you took ages to get here.'

Emmie lowered her voice - 'What if I told you that I just ran into that man I met last night again?'

'So?'

'So... He knows all about us.'

'What do you mean?'

Emmie looked around before answering - 'Like the Blitz.'

Jack's face turned as pale as the table covering, then he looked up at Emmie and forced a laugh - 'Yeah, right... Nice try.'

She fixed him with a level gaze - 'Straight up - that's what he said.'

'Well, I hope you asked him for a route home,' joked Jack. 'Might as well have got something useful out of him.'

'Jack - I'm being serious,' snapped Emmie - her tone getting his attention. 'Apparently, in London we managed to do something which upset the fabric of time, and it needs repairing.' Ordinarily, this would have sounded crazy, but somehow the events which had happened to them since yesterday made it slightly more believable.

'I wonder what we did?' Jack mused. 'We tried to be so careful of the butterfly effect, but I guess we don't really know anything about the rules of time travel.' He sat back and sighed - 'I don't suppose your new friend told you how we're supposed to repair time...?'

'He just said we needed to save Mary,' replied Emmie. Remembering the odd behaviour of her watch, she rolled her sleeve up to show Jack. 'And this has been stuck on 24:00 since yesterday - in the middle of the night it started counting down.'

Jack looked at her wrist - '18:05 - what does that mean? It's the morning, not the evening.'

'Eighteen hours until Titanic sinks,' said Emmie sadly. 'We've got to save Mary - whatever that means - and find our way home before then...'

Time For A Swim?

'I thought Mary was meeting us down here in the dining room?' Emmie peered past Jack and through the open doorway. 'Doesn't look like she's here yet, does it?'

'No - and I'm pretty sure she hasn't been down at all,' replied Jack. 'I've been here for a while, and I haven't seen her.'

'I wonder where she might have got to?' Emmie was keen to help the girl find her brothers, but what had started as a kind act seemed like it might be more important than they thought. 'I think there's a general room up on C deck for the 3rd class passengers - we could try there,' Emmie suggested after a pause. In truth, she was quite bemused at why the girl and her family hadn't appeared - everyone had to eat, after all.

Jack stood up from the table and headed for the stairs - Emmie following behind. 'Is it straight up the staircase at the end?'

'Yes, just keep going,' she confirmed.

At the top, they emerged outside the general room and noticed that the entranceway also led out onto a small promenade deck. Jack peered through the glazed door and noticed that a few people were outside.

'Looks cold,' he observed. The deck area was covered in wooden planks, and two large crane arms sat motionless either side of the ship. Presumably these were for loading cargo on and off in port.

'Come on,' Emmie tugged his arm, 'the general room is through here.' She pushed open the door and went inside.

There were quite a lot of people in the room now - in direct contrast to when Emmie had charged up the stairs earlier that morning. Groups of passengers sat around reading and playing games, and there was a moderate level of background chatter. Emmie scanned the room, but there was no sign of Mary or her family. Disappointed, she sat down on a bench and stared morosely out of the window. 'I can't think where they might have gone,' she admitted to Jack.

A few moments later, a tall man strode into the room, followed by a woman and five children. One of the girls shouted 'Emmie,' and ran across the room to the pair.

'Hello Mary,' smiled Emmie in relief, 'where have you been?'

'Father wanted us to report John and Patrick missing this morning - it's been a whole day now,' she explained. 'We all had to go and see the purser together.'

'Was he able to help?' Jack asked.

'Not really,' she ventured after a small pause. 'He took down their descriptions but pointed out there wasn't anywhere for them to get off until we arrive in New York, so not to be that concerned.' She turned to Emmie - 'I'm so worried about them though - what if they fall overboard?'

'I'm sure they won't do anything that daft,' smiled Emmie, 'we're happy to help you look again - Jack's not in the kitchens this morning.'

'Oh, thank you,' she said, her face breaking into a grin. It would be nice to get out and explore the ship some more, and Emmie was quite bold about going into the places where 3rd class passengers normally weren't allowed. She looked over at her parents, who were now deep in conversation - 'Let's go.'

*

'Where are we going to look first?' asked Emmie, as they left the room and emerged back into the entrance space. Jack was looking excitedly out at the deck, where some younger children were sliding around on the frosty surface. She laughed - 'I don't think we need to look out there - you can see the whole area from here!'

'I think there's a swimming pool towards the front of the ship - that might be worth a look,' Jack explained. 'I'd like to play there if I didn't have anything better to do.'

'John and Patrick can't swim,' admitted Mary, 'but they might like splashing about. How do we get there?'

Emmie nudged Jack and whispered quietly - 'Good idea - definitely a place you wouldn't think of looking.'

'You can get to most places on the ship from the service corridor on E deck,' Jack told them both. 'It's what the crew use, and it runs the length of the ship.' He led the way back down the stairs, emerging near a small cluster of 3rd class cabins. 'It's this way,' he indicated, turning right and pointing to a wide corridor which stretched into the distance. Jack wasn't wrong when he said that the crew used this space to get around - it was heaving with people carrying provisions and moving between different areas of Titanic.

As they rounded a corner where the ship's structure stuck out, the engine noise noticeably increased and Jack encouraged Mary to touch the smooth, metal wall. 'It's warm,' he explained, 'the engines must be behind there.' A number of men wearing overalls came out of a room opposite, carrying bags of tools. 'Look - the engineers are off to work. I hope that doesn't mean there's anything wrong with the ship...' Jack joked but then realised that the timing might not be so funny, given which day it was.

Near the end of the corridor, Emmie paused at a door marked 'Port use only'. 'This is where we were yesterday,' she said thoughtfully, resting a hand on the handle.

'Remind me what's through there?' Jack asked.

'There are some 1st class cabins on that side of the ship.'

'Let's go then,' said Jack eagerly, 'the pool is bound to be in the 1st class part of the ship.'

'Ought we to?' asked Mary quietly. 'It does say it's only to be used in port.'

'Was it open before?' Jack was rarely bothered by rules and was quite happy to ignore the sign.

Emmie nodded and slowly turned the handle. The door opened and she peered left and right quickly, before giving a quick smile and stepping through. Jack followed immediately, but Mary hung back.

'Come on Mary!' hissed Jack, 'someone will notice otherwise.'

Mary looked doubtful but stepped through the doorway and then gasped at the difference on the other side of the thin metal wall. This was like another world to the girl who was travelling in 3rd class - carved wooden panelling everywhere and a deep pile carpet disappearing up the staircase. 'Oh my...' she managed - her eyes bulging at the opulent surroundings.

'Come on!' Jack hissed again, already a few steps down the staircase. 'I bet the pool is down here.' He quickly covered the remaining steps down to a corridor, with doors off to each side. 'Which one?' he mused, eventually deciding the door on the right was the most likely. 'Are you coming in?' he asked - Emmie and Mary having caught him up by this point.

Without waiting for an answer, Jack pushed the door open and disappeared inside. A few moments passed, then there was a loud shout from the other side of the door, and Jack came rushing out.

'Run!' he said breathlessly, grabbing each of their arms and dragging them back along the corridor and through a door at the end. It led into a linen store with large cupboards and floor to ceiling doors.

'What's going on?' Emmie demanded, as Jack stopped to catch his breath. He was panting and laughing at the same time, and his face had gone as red as a beetroot. In between gasps, he was just about able to blurt out an answer.

'It's ladies only...' he managed, chuckling. 'It wasn't the pool either... It was the Turkish baths!'

Emmie and Mary stared at him, not quite understanding what was so funny.

'They didn't have any clothes on!' Jack finished, with a smirk.

Emmie smiled at the ridiculousness of it all, and Mary gasped in horror. 'What - no clothes at all?!' she asked in a shocked voice.

Jack was still smirking, and Emmie aimed a gentle punch at him - 'Jack! Not clever.' At that moment, they became aware of loud footsteps walking in the corridor outside the door, and Jack quickly pulled them into one of the cupboards and swung the door closed. They were just in time, as the outer door opened, and two angry sounding women came into the room.

'Did you see where those children went?' said one crossly.

'I thought they came through here, but they must have run off up the stairs,' answered the other. 'The parents must be letting them run wild - don't they know this is out of bounds to children?' After a few moments grumbling, the pair departed and left the room in silence once more.

In the gloom of the cupboard, the trio looked at each other - 'Well, I guess that answers the question as to whether Patrick and John are down here,' said Emmie. 'They'd stand out like a sore thumb.'

'What are we going to do now?' asked Mary. She was terrified of being caught in the wrong area of the ship and getting into trouble, yet captivated by this other world that people on the same journey inhabited.

'Just wait a minute,' advised Jack quietly, putting a finger to his lips. 'We need to make sure they're not going to come back first.' After a few further moments in the darkness, it seemed that they were going to remain alone, and Jack eased the door open, peeking around it into the main part of the linen store. 'All clear,' he said with a certain amount of relief - not wanting to get caught out either.

'Those women seemed to suggest there were more stairs through here,' pointed out Emmie - indicating a small door at the end of the room. They followed her across to it and quietly tip-toed through - it led to a larger room where Jack's nose told him the dirty linen was stored.

'Phwoar,' he grumbled, 'it stinks in here!' He looked around, staring at a large opening, high up on the wall. 'I've been in here before,' he exclaimed, 'this is where the laundry chute I slid down came out!'

'What do you mean?' asked Mary, looking confused at the conversation which passed between them.

'Long story,' smiled Jack, 'but basically I slid down from the deck above, and in through that hole up there.'

Mary's mouth made a little 'O' of surprise - these two got up to some really strange things.

'Anyway,' Jack went on, 'there's a door to the side which leads back up again.' He pointed to a door on the far side of the room - it seemed like the ship was full of them - which led into a passage with a narrow staircase at the end. 'Result!' Jack said excitedly and led the way to the stairs. They were poorly lit, and their footsteps echoed on the metal treads as they ascended.

'Quieten down a bit,' suggested Emmie, feeling a lot less gung-ho than Jack was appearing to be. She was nervous about their impending deadline and didn't want to get into any trouble that might distract from it. Jack turned and stuck his tongue out at her - he was clearly pleased with himself at knowing their escape route.

As they reached the top of the stairs, a strange sight greeted them. A row of basins stretched out across the wall, running the length of it, and there was a slightly unpleasant aroma in the air. Jack looked uncomfortable - this wasn't what he'd been expecting.

'Are we...? Is this a... bathroom?' asked Mary in surprise.

They got their answer a few seconds later, when there was the distinct sound of a toilet flushing from the right, and a large man emerged, tucking his shirt back into his trousers. 'What do you think you're doing in here?!' he said angrily, taking a step towards them.

Locked In

Jack's eyes widened as he turned to face the man and realised that it was the purser - Mr Barrow. There was a momentary flash of confusion on the purser's face, and then his features came together in a snarl - he had definitely recognised Jack. 'What are you doing away from the kitchen again?' he demanded.

Taking half a step back, Jack weighed up his options and decided that they were very limited. If he tried to run from the room - either through the door or back down the stairs - the chances were that Emmie and Mary would get the full force of the man's anger. He stood silently for a moment.

'Well?' insisted Mr Barrow, 'I haven't got all day...'

'Sorry...' began Jack, 'we were just exploring...' He didn't get any further with his explanation, as he found himself being quickly propelled out of the room - a large hand on his shoulder for the second time in two days.

'You two as well,' he ordered the girls. 'I'll deal with you later.' As they exited the bathroom into the corridor, Mr Barrow swiftly stepped across to another door, took out a key from a large bunch in his pocket, and unlocked it. 'Inside,' he said gruffly, motioning at Emmie and Mary.

They walked hesitantly towards the door - it led into a dark space which looked rather like a storeroom. 'Please...' begged Mary, 'we weren't doing any harm.'

'Snooping around might not seem like a problem to you but it might to our... *better class* passengers,' he replied snootily. 'Now get in there and keep the noise down.'

Mary started to sniff a little, and Emmie looked daggers at the man. 'You can't lock us up,' she muttered, though she knew where this was heading.

'Watch me,' he said, clearly losing patience with the pair. With that, he gave Emmie a little shove, and shut the door behind both girls, locking it and pocketing the key. Jack stared at him, aghast.

'Why did you do that?' he asked, feeling a wave of helplessness wash over him. This was just like yesterday - now he was going to have to find Emmie all over again, and time was not on their side.

'That's enough from you - you're going back to the kitchen, and this time you're going to stay there.' Leading him back down the corridor, Mr Barrow took great delight in giving Jack a nudge as they passed any of the crew. It was his way of reminding everyone who was in charge, and almost daring them to challenge him.

Once they got towards the rear of the ship and had taken the stairs back up to the main kitchen on D deck, Mr Barrow handed Jack over to one of the chefs, who was making a start on lunch. 'Don't let this one out of your sight,' he said firmly, 'he's trouble and he's going to stay in here until this evening.'

*

Back downstairs in the storeroom, Emmie had worked out that there was a light, but couldn't find the switch. The walls all seemed to be covered in some kind of racking, and there were stacks of boxes and what felt like assorted tools lying about. After running her hands along each wall in turn - no mean feat when they were mostly obscured with shelves - she managed to touch what felt like a light switch. The trouble was it sat behind a really heavy metal box wedged tightly onto one of the shelves. Between her and Mary, they eventually managed to inch the box far enough forward to slip a hand between the back of it and the wall. Emmie's fingers stretched and just managed to flick the switch.

For a moment there was nothing, and then a bare bulb above their heads started humming and slowly began to glow. It wasn't a bright light, even after a couple of minutes when it should really have warmed up. Looking around the room, they could see that it was probably a tradesperson's storage cupboard - there were a lot of hand tools on the shelves, and the boxes all seemed to contain metal fittings and lengths of pipe.

Mary sniffed a bit more - 'We're going to be in so much trouble when that man comes back.'

Emmie looked around the room, trying to size it up. 'Not if I can help it,' she said grimly, 'I'm not intending for us to still be in here.'

'What do you mean?' Mary asked, looking confused, 'you heard him lock the door.'

'Look up there,' pointed Emmie. She had seen a small ventilation grille, half hidden behind one of the shelving units, high up on the wall. 'I reckon we can fit through that.'

'But... It's so high...' stammered Mary, 'how will we get up there?'

'That's the easy part - these shelves will make a good ladder.' Emmie took some items off the lower layers to make a bit more space, and then started to climb the racking. When she reached the grille, she tried to look through, but the mesh covering it was too fine. 'It seems to be screwed on,' she called down to Mary, 'can you see a screwdriver down there?'

Mary rummaged in some of the boxes and came out with a small, wooden-handled screwdriver. Passing it up to Emmie, she called out, 'Be careful up there.'

Emmie reached back up to the grille and set to work on the screws. The first two came out easily, but the third was really stiff. Moving onto the last one, she undid it and then began to wiggle the grille in an attempt to loosen the stiff screw. It was no good - it seemed well and truly stuck.

'Can you manage it?' asked Mary hopefully.

Emmie gritted her teeth and shook the grille hard. For a moment nothing happened, and then she suddenly felt a strange lightness, immediately followed by a bump as she crashed down onto the floor, twisted grate still in her hand. 'Uhhh,' she groaned, the breath knocked out of her.

'Emmie! Are you alright?' Mary was shocked to see her friend sprawled on the floor.

'Yes... I think so,' came the reply. Emmie sat up, clutching the grille, and looked back at the hole she had uncovered. 'Can you get through there?' she asked. Without waiting for an answer, she was back on her feet and scrambling up the shelving again.

The hole appeared to lead into some sort of air vent pipe - it was shiny and box-shaped, but too dark to see where it went. 'I think we'll fit through,' Emmie confirmed - Mary was smaller than she was, and it looked big enough for her to wriggle into. 'Are you coming?'

'Right behind you,' replied Mary, sounding anything but convinced by this latest plan. She didn't want the man to come back and find them, but the idea of crawling into the pipe was almost as unappealing.

Emmie put the grille down on the top shelf and slid her head and shoulders into the opening. It was a little wider than she was, and movement was possible by bracing her hands against the sides and inching forward. After a few moments of this, she felt her feet on the edge of the hole and then found it much easier to propel herself with both sets of limbs working together.

Once she was fully inside the vent pipe, it was much harder to see anything, as the light from the storeroom was blocked by her body. She moved slowly forward for what seemed like an age, hearing an increase in the ever-present background hum as she passed over what must have been the engine room. Her fingers suddenly touched metal in front of her and, at the same time, a space opened up to the side. Feeling around, she realised that there must be another grille in front of her and that the vent pipe continued round to her right.

She pushed on the grille and found that it was firmly attached - the space behind was dark, as the room it gave onto must be another cupboard of sorts. What to do now? Emmie tried to think what Jack might do in a similar position - he was more impulsive than her, and this situation felt like it needed less caution and more action. An idea suddenly popped into her head, and she worked her body around the bend in the pipe so that her feet were now level with the grille.

Stretching out her legs, she pushed on the grille with as much strength as she could muster - feeling it flex but not give. It was something though - the grille wasn't immoveable. She tried again; this time sure that it didn't spring back as far as it had initially. A couple more pushes and then she started to doubt her plan - flexing was one thing, but it wouldn't help her get out of here. In frustration, she pulled her legs back and brought her heels down hard on the grille. There was a screeching noise, and one corner of it popped out and stayed there. Elated, but also aware this latest approach was quite noisy, Emmie tried to time her kicks with the engine note from somewhere underneath her. Whether that was successful or not she wasn't sure but, after several stout kicks, the grille flew off and landed in the room beyond with a clang.

'Mary are you ok?' she called quietly, hoping that the girl had managed to climb into the vent by herself. There was no response, though Emmie could hear a faint whimpering noise coming from the right direction. 'Mary?' she called again, still getting no answer. Needing to see what was happening further back in the pipe, Emmie wriggled forward to get her legs out of the newly opened hole. As her waist reached the exit, she twisted around onto her stomach to allow her legs to hopefully reach something to stand on. There was nothing. She swung her legs left and right, hoping to reach something firm but, in the end, had to drop to the floor blindly.

The room was really dark, but had a familiar smell of clean laundry and, as she felt around the walls, this was confirmed by piles of folded linen. There was a light switch by the door, and the bulb shone brightly as she turned it on, causing her to blink after so long in the dark. Looking back at the hole, she saw that the grille had been on the only part of the wall not covered in shelves containing stacked bedding. There was an Ottoman chest in one corner of the room, and Emmie pushed it over to the grille opening, enabling her to stand and look back into the vent.

'Mary,' she called once more, 'are you in there?' There was some movement, and then a small voice answered her.

'I'm here. I don't like it though.'

'Oh, well done - you're almost at the end,' Emmie said encouragingly, though the truth was she couldn't see the girl yet to know. She put her arm into the vent pipe and waved it around. 'Reach out for me - I'll pull you through.'

After a brief pause, Emmie could feel Mary's small hand groping around in front of her and stretched to touch it. 'Aargh!' squealed Mary, 'what was that?!'

'It's me, silly!' replied Emmie, 'I told you I'd pull you the last little bit.' She reached for Mary's hand again and grasped it firmly. Pulling the girl through the pipe was actually quite easy, although Mary's eyes nearly popped out of her head when she emerged face down to the floor. 'You've just got to trust me,' Emmie explained, 'wriggle out to your waist and then I'll support you the rest of the way.'

Some contortion and a bit more squealing later, the girls were both sitting on the Ottoman, looking around the room. 'How do we get out of here, then?' Mary enquired, 'that door is probably locked too...' Just as Emmie was about to answer, the pair heard footsteps outside, and the light suddenly went off. Suppressing a cry of surprise, Emmie pulled Mary down from the Ottoman, lifted the lid and bundled her inside. They lay together in the large chest, breathing heavily and wondering what was about to happen.

How The Other Half Live

At first there was silence, then the girls heard the scraping sound of a key being placed into a lock, and a slight creak as the door opened. A click followed, then a pause and a series of further clicks, before silence descended once more. Emmie waited a moment, before inching the lid of the Ottoman up, and peering out.

'What can you see?' Mary whispered, her voice sounding much louder in the confines of the chest.

Emmie raised the lid a bit higher. 'Nothing,' she said, 'it's too dark in here.' Taking a chance, she pushed the lid fully open - the room appeared to be empty but there was no saying when the person who had entered might return.

'What happened? Why do you think they went away?'

'I think the light must have broken - the bulb maybe - whoever came in tried the switch a few times and gave up,' Emmie explained, feeling a little elated at the possibility of an easy exit now. 'I don't think they locked the door again either.'

Both girls climbed out of the chest and walked over to the door. Emmie pressed her ear to it, trying to listen for any noises from whatever was beyond. There was just silence, so she gently tried the handle and was pleased to find that the door swung open easily - leading out onto a carpeted corridor. Looking out, Emmie realised that they were now in the 1st class part of the ship.

'Come on - you'll never believe this...' she encouraged Mary, opening the door wider to let the other girl look too.

Mary's eyes bulged, and her jaw noticeably dropped. The corridor alone was much fancier than anything she had ever seen before - a deep red carpet ran along its length, with polished wooden handrails at waist height on the white painted panelling. There were pairs of brass double wall lights on every other panel, and the overall impression was of total sophistication.

'Want to have a quick look around?' suggested Emmie, smoothing her hair and blouse down. It wouldn't do to wander around this part of the ship looking like you had just crawled out of a ventilation pipe! Mary nodded apprehensively and did the same, following Emmie out of the linen room and into the corridor.

Emmie looked left and right, realising that they were near the end of the corridor, and decided to take a chance and let Mary see how these passengers lived.

'Are you sure?' Mary felt uneasy in this space yet fascinated at the same time.

'It's quiet - I think everyone's probably at lunch. This is as good a time as we're going to get.' Mary agreed and followed Emmie along the hallway, looking with interest at the space between each door.

'Are the cabins really that big?' she asked in surprise. The doors were spaced at least twice as far apart as on the lower decks.

'See for yourself,' Emmie replied with a grin, as they passed the open door of a room being cleaned by the housekeepers. Mary stared incredulously at the cabin's interior - dark panelling, carved wooden bedstead and dressing table alongside - it was a world away from her own cabin, with ten bunks crammed into a space less than half the size. 'The cabins on the higher decks are even larger,' Emmie explained, 'some of them have separate sitting rooms too.' Feeling mischievous, she added - 'Want to have a proper look inside this room?'

Mary looked at her with a mixture of shock and awe - 'Really? What, actually inside?'

'Sure - why not? We'll have to be quick, but it looks like the housekeepers are at lunch too...' Emmie checked back down the corridor and then stepped into the bedroom. There was a heavily perfumed aroma, and she could see various trinkets laid out on the dressing table - a silver hairbrush and a hand mirror. 'Come on in,' she called to Mary, 'it's ok - no-one will know.'

In the end, she had to go back and drag the girl over the threshold, so nervous was she about getting into trouble. Once inside though, Mary looked around in wonder - she knew the ship was large, and that her family had the cheapest class of travel, but had never expected such a gulf.

'I wonder how the bed feels...' said Emmie, with a glint in her eye. 'Shall we find out?'

'No - you mustn't—' Mary's voice had taken a horrified tone. Emmie took no notice though and lay down across the bed.

'Mmm,' she said contentedly, 'this is amazing!' She waved Mary over to join her - 'You've got to try it too!'

Mary shook her head, thinking this was probably too far. 'Come on,' she pleaded, 'I think we should go now...'

Emmie sat up, bounced a few times on the luxuriously soft bed, and reluctantly agreed. 'Ok, I guess we probably should - lovely bed though!'

As they left the room, Mary thought about what kind of life might be waiting for her when they reached America. It was almost as if Emmie could read her mind, as she turned to the girl and asked - 'How different do you think America will be to what you're used to?'

'Father says we'll live in New York to start with,' Mary replied, 'he says it's a big city, and I don't think it will be like our old life at all. We lived in a little cottage on the farm where Father worked.'

'That sounds like a big change,' admitted Emmie, 'what's the furthest you've been before?'

'How far from home, do you mean?'

'Yes - apart from right now of course,' Emmie joked.

'Probably market day in Tallow - it was the nearest town.' Mary looked wistful for a moment - 'I don't suppose I'll ever see Ireland again...'

Emmie gulped, suddenly feeling very responsible for the girl. She really liked Mary, even before the mysterious man had explained that they somehow had to save her. It wasn't quite clear what they had to save her from, but every passing hour made it seem more likely that it would be Titanic's terrible end that was the biggest risk to Mary. She discreetly checked her watch and, to her horror, saw that it read 12:17 - time was running short...

*

Jack, meanwhile, was having a far less interesting time. When Mr Barrow had left him in the kitchen with strict instructions not to leave before the dinner service was finished, the chefs who were present rubbed their hands together in delight. Another helper to prepare lunch before the rest of the kitchen team arrived was not to be sniffed at.

'Right then,' said one of them, as Jack put on a clean jacket and apron, 'it's Cockie Leekie today, so you can start by chopping the leeks.' He gestured towards the vegetable preparation room in the corner where, to Jack's dismay, he could see several stacked boxes of leeks on the floor. Walking into the room, he noticed that there was a chopping board and knife already laid out, and a further stack of leeks at the end of the bench. 'Put them straight in the stock pot,' the man called after him.

Jack looked over at the large steam powered stock pot - it was huge and would take all the leeks he could see and more. Sighing to himself, he picked up the knife and his first leek, and started chopping. It had probably taken him at least half an hour to get through the stack of boxes on the floor, when the rest of the kitchen workers started to file in. Jack's mood lifted at this point as company would mean the job felt less tedious, though still likely to take as long.

A few other boys joined him to prepare the vegetable selection for lunch, and one showed him how to use the waste chute in the corner of the kitchen. It was like a giant metal bin that you loaded up and then pulled a lever to empty. Jack had asked where the rubbish went and was startled to discover that it was shot out of the side of Titanic into the sea, blasted by a jet of steam!

The chef who had been asked to keep an eye on Jack did exactly that and, before long, he found himself collecting cheese from the giant hoist just outside the kitchen. He didn't mind this task, as he was allowed to carry the whole cheeses from the hoist and collect them on a table in the kitchen, before cutting a thick slice out to display the cheese inside. The cheeses were arranged on a series of trollies, ready to be pushed into the dining room once the main part of the lunch was over.

As the diners filled up the grand room beyond the kitchen and food started to be ferried out, the mood relaxed temporarily. This was the lull where the workers could grab a bite to eat, and a giant plate of sandwiches appeared in the middle of the room for exactly this purpose. The bakers always made a surplus of bread, to ensure the kitchen staff could eat on the go and therefore not waste any time.

As the dirty dishes started to come back in from the dining room, Jack seized an opportunity to continue fetching and carrying from the hoist. There was a shortage of Stilton cheese on the trollies, as not much had been sent up with the rest of the cheeses. A few waiters came through asking for more and Jack put his hand up to collect it. He was given a note to send down in the hoist and headed out of the kitchen.

As he reached the hoist, he found that the sliding steel mesh doors across the front were closed, and it appeared to be on a deck below. Jack noticed a metal tube on the side of the door, which had a funnel shaped end. 'You talk into that, mate,' said a passing sailor - pointing at the tube.

'Thanks,' replied Jack, picking up the tube and wondering what to say. 'Umm, I need some cheese...' he started. There was a pause as he waited for a reply.

'What's that?' came a distorted voice from the other end of the tube.

'I. Need. Some. More. Stilton.' Jack tried to enunciate his request clearly.

'How much?'

This was tricky - no-one had said exactly how much was needed. 'Four cheeses,' he guessed in reply. There was a longer pause, and then he heard the hoist whir into action. The cargo bay rose up in front of him and he slid the mesh doors open - inside were four enormous cylinders of cheese, wrapped in greaseproof paper. He tried to pick up the first one and staggered a little - it was really heavy. This wasn't looking like the easy job he'd expected it to be.

Steadying himself, he made his way back to the kitchen, where a grateful waiter took it from him. He then returned to the hoist, this time noticing a man in a dark overcoat standing nearby. As he approached, the man looked up and greeted him warmly.

'Hello Jack,' he said, smiling, 'how are you getting on? I hope you've found what you were looking for?'

Before waiting for an answer, the man nodded at Jack and walked past him, down the corridor. Confused, Jack turned to watch him go, thinking it was odd that no-one else seemed to notice the man as he strode away. He presumed it was yet another case of mistaken identity, so continued carrying the rest of the cheese back to the kitchen.

He couldn't quite reach the last wheel of cheese by leaning through the open door, so he stepped into the hoist briefly to pick it up. As he bent down in the cavity, the floor lurched and Jack grabbed at the door to steady himself. This action caused the mesh to slide closed and the hoist began to glide down into the darkness. Someone must have called it from the storeroom below. 'Stop!' cried Jack, only able to half stand up and fearing the hoist wasn't strong enough to take his weight. 'Stop - I'm stuck in here...'

The Boat Deck

As they left the bedroom, glad that it was still quiet in the corridor outside, Emmie racked her brain thinking about where Mary's brothers might be. She couldn't work out whether the lost boys were key to their task of 'saving' Mary but could imagine that their absence would complicate things at some point.

'Seeing as we're up here - shall we try and have a look at the lifeboats in case your brothers are playing hide and seek?' Emmie asked.

'Yes - that's a good idea. Where are they?' Mary replied. The ship was so huge that she was feeling a little disorientated with each new area they passed through.

'Up another couple of decks.' Emmie was keen to move sooner rather than later and led them round a corner where they saw a row of polished doors opposite them. One was open, with a smartly suited boy inside - his black jacket decorated with a row of gold buttons.

'What are these?' Mary whispered to Emmie.

'It's a lift - like yesterday,' Emmie whispered back, walking confidently inside, and asking for C deck. The attendant looked curiously at the girls, seeming to question whether they should be there, but Emmie smiled sweetly at him and, after a pause, he pressed the button, causing the doors to slide shut.

Mary's legs almost gave way at the surprise of the lift's motion, and Emmie quickly put an arm around the girl to steady her. The lift attendant was still looking them with an air of suspicion, and Emmie was glad when the lift stopped two decks up from their starting point.

'Thank you,' she said, as the girls exited the car and found themselves in a large reception area. They quickly walked away from the lift, and Emmie saw that backing onto the lift shaft was a grand staircase, similar to the one they had seen when arriving on the ship.

Although they were a deck lower, Emmie's thoughts flashed back to the door which led to the present, and the awareness of passing time nagged at her. 'Let's take the stairs,' she suggested, keen to try and find Patrick and John as quickly as possible.

They quickly climbed the next couple of flights of stairs, trying to avoid unnecessary eye contact with passengers going the other way. As they reached A deck, the stairs opened out into a large open space, and Emmie steered Mary away from the final flight and across the room to a door in the corner. She pushed it open and stepped out on to the covered deck outside.

'There were a few too many people in there,' she explained to Mary, 'we'd be better off going the rest of the way outside.' Walking quickly in the cold air, the girls soon found a staircase going up to the boat deck and clattered up - grateful for having got this far unchallenged.

'We're at the top,' breathed Mary in wonder, as they emerged onto the boat deck, with nothing above them except the grey sky and a streaming trail of smoke from the engine room. Looking up at the nearest funnel, angled back towards them and painted buff with a black band, it was hard not to feel small - so gigantic were the structures.

'The very top,' smiled Emmie. There was quite a breeze out here as the ship ploughed through the sea, and it blew the length of the deck right at them. 'Let's have a look at these lifeboats, now we're here.'

A little further back from where they had emerged, hung four shiny white boats, suspended from their cranes above the deck, and angled slightly over the side. Looking further along, the same number were in the forward section of the deck too. Emmie took a step towards the lifeboats, intending to see if they could look under the covers.

'They're quite high up, aren't they?' Mary wondered out loud. The boats were resting on large blocks on the deck surface, and their sides were so tall that the girls couldn't see over them. There were canvas covers pulled tight and held down with cord around the edges.

'I think an adult would struggle to get into these without a step, let alone your brothers.' Emmie studied the cord securing the covers as she said this. 'I don't think anyone could tie the covers down from the inside either.' Wanting to be sure, she walked over to the first lifeboat, knocking on the side as she went.

Mary joined her - 'Patrick? John?' she called as they knocked. There was no answer, so they moved onto the next boat. Suddenly, Emmie looked up - the man who had told her about the time rift stood tucked out of sight between two lifeboats. He raised a finger to his lips and Emmie paused, allowing Mary to carry on along the row of boats.

The man studied her for a moment, seeming to take in a lot from her demeanour. 'Be careful not to remove anything from the ship which belongs here,' he said quietly.

'What do you mean? And what was that earlier about saving Mary?' Emmie hissed, keeping one eye on the girl in front.

'Did you say something?' Mary called, turning back to look at Emmie.

The man shook his head slowly, pointing downwards and then put his finger to his lips once more. She quickly shifted her gaze away and walked after Mary - frustrated that she hadn't had time to get a reply. What could he mean about taking things from the ship? She hadn't - had she?

'What were you doing?' asked Mary.

'Just thinking...' answered Emmie, 'I can't see how your brothers would be inside any of these boats.' She looked at Mary - 'I think we've done all we can on these upper decks. I wonder if we need to go right back down and start at the bottom?' The man seemed to have indicated she should go down, so that's what they would do.

'What, the engine room?' asked Mary in surprise. She'd lived with the ever-present drone of the engines since they'd boarded Titanic - they were noisy enough at the cabin level, let alone how she imagined they might be in the engine room itself. 'Do you think we'll be able to get in there?'

'I don't honestly know,' replied Emmie, 'but it will give us a good idea of whether John and Patrick might have been able to slip inside. They would probably be curious to see the engines.'

'How will we find our way in? It's probably not signposted.' Mary made a good point - the areas of the ship which were 'crew only' wouldn't be made obvious to the travelling public.

'We should start back down on the deck where we got shut into that cupboard,' suggested Emmie, 'it seemed to have a lot of the ship's crew facilities down there.'

Mary's face fell at this point and her hand started to shake. The idea of running into the man who had locked them in again filled her with dread. 'Do we have to?' she whispered.

*

Going down the stairs back down to E deck, Emmie and Mary both wondered what they might find. Despite the urgency, Emmie was a little bit excited to see the scale of the engines which powered this gigantic ship, and Mary was fervently hoping that they would be able to get in and out without seeing any of the crew.

They emerged out onto the wide service corridor which they had walked along earlier, and fairly soon after passed through a large metal sliding door. It stood the full width of the corridor and appeared to sit on a track of some sort. There was a sign stencilled on it which read 'WT Door No. 36'.

'Let's hope these watertight doors never get used,' remarked Mary. The doors had been designed to contain flooding if the ship was damaged and were one of the main reasons it had a reputation as unsinkable. Emmie shuddered to herself - little did the girl know that they would be closed for real that very day.

Stepping over the lip of the door, they continued along the corridor, noticing most of the cabins were marked for the ship's workers. There also seemed to be quite a large number of toilets, as there was a tell-tale aroma coming from behind some of the doors.

Rounding a corner, the girls struck lucky - a door opened ahead of them, and out stepped a man in some dirty white overalls, carrying a bag of tools in his hand. He carefully shut the door behind him and started along the corridor away from them.

Almost immediately, they saw him stand to the side as a group of men strode in their direction. They were led by a man with a white beard and four gold stripes on the cuffs of his dark jacket. The others following behind were deep in discussion; pointing out various things as they walked along.

Emmie and Mary watched as the engineer pulled himself up straight against the corridor wall as the group passed. 'Captain,' he said to the leading man, who nodded a greeting in reply.

Emmie tugged Mary's arm - 'Along here,' she hissed, pulling the girl into an alcove just past where they stood. They waited quietly for the group to pass them, hearts beating quickly in anticipation.

'How are the engines running, Chief?' came a voice from around the corner. Emmie couldn't catch what was said and shuffled closer to the corner to hear better. She braved a peek back at the group of men and saw that the captain was talking to the engineer. 'Do you think they're ready for a speed run?' he asked.

The engineer's reply seemed to be positive, as the captain looked pleased with it, adding, 'Can't let Cunard have it all their own way, can we?'

Ducking back, as the captain started along the corridor again, Emmie wondered about what she had heard. She knew Titanic sank after hitting an iceberg, but had they been trying to set a speed record too?

The men passed, and Emmie counted a few seconds in her head before stepping back out into the walkway. 'Come on,' she said to Mary, 'let's see where that door leads to.' Mary still looked uncomfortable but followed behind anyway. Placing a hand on the door handle, Emmie jumped back when it appeared to turn by itself, swinging open and leaving them face to face with the man in the dark coat from the boat deck.

It was hard to tell who was more surprised, but the man reacted fastest, saying sharply, 'What are you doing? This area is out of bounds to passengers.' He showed no sign of recognising Emmie, and just stared the pair down.

'Umm,' Emmie stuttered, 'sorry...' Her shoulders slumped in defeat, and she turned to Mary - 'Let's go.' Mary wasn't sure whether to be relieved or disappointed - she hadn't really wanted to explore the engine room but was desperate to find her brothers.

Retreating back down the corridor, Emmie half-turned to look at the man. He was watching them go - but how had he got down here so quickly? They had left the boat deck as soon as Emmie had finished talking to him and come straight down the stairs.

Emmie thought for a moment, as they walked back to the rear of the ship together - 'I'm not sure we've got many places left to look for your brothers... They've probably been moving about the ship anyway - trying to avoid getting spotted.'

Mary nodded sadly - she'd reached the same conclusion herself. 'I'd probably better get back and see if Father has had any news. Hopefully, the crew are keeping an eye out for them now, since he reported them missing.'

'Ok - I'll try and find you later - where do you think you'll be?'

'Probably the general room,' replied Mary, 'that's where Father likes us to spend the evening.'

The Hoist

Trapped in the rapidly descending lift car, Jack braced himself against the sides and closed his eyes. He shouldn't have stepped inside, but it had seemed the easiest way of reaching the Stilton wheel. The cheese was imminently going to be splattered all over the roof, along with him, unless a miracle happened.

As he waited for the seemingly inevitable impact, the car began to shudder and screech. Was it slowing? Opening one eye, Jack could see sparks raining in through the mesh side as metal rubbed on metal in the hoist shaft. There was a definite sensation of slowing down though, and Jack opened his other eye and began to hope a little again.

SLAM! The car hit the base of the shaft, sending Jack crashing to the ground in a heap. There was shouting from outside, and a large hand dragged the hoist door open. Jack lifted his head from the greasy metal floor, realising slowly that he was curled up, hugging the wheel of Stilton.

'Come here, lad!' an arm reached in to help him to his feet and Jack staggered out, his legs feeling like they were made of rubber. 'What happened?' asked the same voice - it belonged to a tall man with tattooed arms and a cap pushed back on his head. 'Why were you in there?'

Jack tried to explain that he had been unloading the cheese and stepped in, causing the hoist to fall. He thought he was going to get into trouble, but the man looked concerned instead. 'Are you alright? Just shocked I suppose?' Turning to another sailor stood behind him, the man said, 'The hoist should be rated for more weight than that - call an engineer, will you?'

Sitting Jack down on a closed packing case, he instructed the boy to rest quietly for a few minutes. Jack's shoulder hurt a bit, but he felt a lot better than he had dared to hope. When the hoist started to plummet, he had feared the worst - the few seconds in freefall seeming to last forever. It sounded like there was a problem with the hoist - that was probably a good thing from his point of view, as it might save him getting into any further trouble with Mr Barrow when he returned to the kitchen.

As Jack gazed around, he could see a large platform across to his right, with a long row of what looked like instruments and switches mounted on it. Intrigued, he stared across, seeing a small, balding man occasionally moving one of the switches, which would then give off crackling blue sparks as it was actioned.

'Feeling better then?' - the man who had helped him was back. 'We'd better get you up to the kitchen if you're alright.'

Jack pointed at the platform - 'What's that?' He might be about to be sent back to work, but his curiosity was aroused now.

'The switchboard,' came the reply, 'controls all of the electricity around the ship.' He started towards the stairs - 'Come on then.' Jack paused to look back over his shoulder at the array of switches - fascinated by their complexity. He strained to see how far they stretched into the distance but was hailed from the bottom of the stairs - 'I said - come on!'

They walked up the steps together, the cramped and narrow staircase passing through the storage area on G deck, before emerging back out by the damaged hoist entrance. Jack noticed that a team of engineers were already busy inspecting the hoist machinery.

Allowing himself to be led into the kitchen, Jack looked cautiously around - it looked like the lunch service was over, and the room was a lot quieter. 'There you are... What happened to that cheese?' - he was approached by the chef who had been charged with keeping an eye on him. The man from the storeroom stepped in and explained what had happened - causing the chef's demeanour to soften slightly.

'Right then - you can help with preparing the desserts for later. Should be a nice easy job for you.' He pointed through to the pastry kitchen - 'You'll find the ingredients laid out on the side, along with the recipe.'

As Jack walked through the doorway, his thoughts turned to Emmie. Hopefully she was having a better time than he was... Once he was let out of the kitchen after dinner, he would head back to the main stairs where she should be waiting for him.

Finding the ingredients and recipe laid out as the chef had said, Jack began to read. 'Waldorf pudding' - he had never heard of it. Seemingly, it was a pudding with apples and grapes in and, just like the soup for lunch, he now had an enormous stack of produce to prepare and chop... Sighing to himself, he picked up the first apple and began to peel it.

*

What felt like an eternity later, Jack had finished chopping fruit and was now helping one of the chefs to spoon the pudding mixture into large moulds. The moulds were placed onto trays, and then into the giant steam ovens in the centre of the kitchen.

'You're on service tonight too,' the chef told him once the puddings were in the oven. 'I've been told to keep you busy.' Jack groaned to himself - there would be no chance of escaping early. He walked back into the main kitchen, hung up his apron and checked his white jacket for stains. There was a small one on the sleeve which he dabbed at with a cloth, largely managing to remove it before he joined the other waiting staff, ready to begin the service.

There was a menu pinned up near the door, showing the order of dishes that evening. Jack skimmed across it - there were eleven courses if you counted the cheese and fruit selection at the end. Eleven! That was insane - who ate that much for their evening meal?!

'Ok, let's go,' one of the waiters announced, and the group started to pick up plates of oysters and other hors d'oeuvres to carry into the dining room. Jack picked up two plates and followed through the door, narrowly avoiding it swinging back into his face from the previous boy's exit.

The grand 1st class dining room set for dinner was every bit as impressive as when he had seen it the day before. The green upholstered chairs arranged around tables weighed down with the best china and silver cutlery looked like they belonged in a palace, rather than on board a ship.

Not realising that he had paused until he was given a nudge in the back by another waiter, did Jack offer his plated starters to a nearby table of guests. All the male passengers were dressed in dinner suits, black bow ties at their throats, and there was an abundance of pearls and the finest silks on display from the ladies present.

Carefully putting his plates of oysters down in the centre of the table, Jack briefly noted that the conversation was centred on the amount of ice in this part of the Atlantic. 'Of course, we'll be fine,' said one man confidently, 'this ship is unsinkable after all.'

Jack retreated to the kitchen, pondering this latest point. He knew this was the night Titanic sank and, that for a lot of these people, this would be their last meal. Suddenly, a wave of sadness washed over him - he knew about the tragedy which would soon unfold yet couldn't do anything about it. The man Emmie had spoken to had suggested something they did in 1940 had caused a problem in time. He couldn't think what it could be, but the idea of making things even worse was too terrible to contemplate. Maybe that was why the tunnel had closed up behind them? Did they have to put right whatever had gone wrong in order to get home?

Knowing that he had to talk to Emmie as soon as he was released, Jack got back to work ferrying out plates of food and collecting empty ones as they were finished with. On one trip back to the kitchen, he noticed that the captain was on his feet pouring wine for the guests on his table. He heard the captain address the man next to him - 'And for you, Mr Guggenheim, sir?' Something clicked in Jack's memory - Guggenheim was the name of a famous museum in New York - maybe this well-dressed man was something to do with it?

Mid-way through the epic meal, after two heavy meat courses, the waiting staff were directed to bring out 'Punch Romaine' - this was a palate cleanser made with wine, rum and champagne, and served in elegant cocktail glasses. Jack picked up a tray of these glasses and gingerly carried them out to the waiting diners. He began placing a glass in front of each person at a large, round table when, without warning, a dark-haired man stood suddenly, knocking into Jack. *CRASH!* went the rest of the glasses on the tray, the contents of at least one finding a new home on the man's dinner jacket.

'You clumsy idiot!' he said angrily, 'look what you've done.'

'I'm so sorry,' mumbled Jack, bending down to try and pick up the broken glass.

'You've ruined my jacket - it's soaking wet.'

Jack was vaguely aware in his flustered state of another waiter coming across to help him. The glass was swept up and he was guided back to the kitchen. 'I think it's best you don't go back out there tonight,' said the head waiter, a grim expression on his face. He was worried about getting a complaint from the passenger and thought removing Jack from the situation might be the best option.

Jack leaned against the wall, his head in his hands. 'I'm sorry,' he said again. Today had been quite a day - getting caught out after looking in the Turkish baths, being banished to the kitchen for the rest of the day, and nearly having a nasty accident in the food hoist. Hopefully spilling a drink on a passenger would be the last bit of bad luck to happen to him. His thoughts quickly returned to the impending fate of Titanic that night though and realised that there was likely more trouble to come unless they got off the ship quickly.

'Right - you can join in with the washing up. Hopefully you can't do too much damage in there,' instructed the head waiter. Jack walked through the kitchen to collect an apron and then headed for the scullery to help wash up.

There was already a full team of people washing dishes and drying them, so Jack collected piles of clean china and ferried them back to the cupboards outside the kitchen. He arranged the delicate plates carefully on the dressers inside the cupboard, ensuring that they were secure against the motion of the ship. Returning to the scullery, he overheard two of the men who were washing up discussing the ship's giant funnels.

'The fourth's not real, you say?' asked one.

'That's right - one of the lads in Engineering told me,' came the reply. 'Apparently, it's used to vent our cooking ranges, amongst other things.' He smiled at this point - it was a common complaint that the kitchens always had a heavy aroma of whatever had been cooking - implying that they weren't that well ventilated after all.

A fake funnel? Jack was interested now - that would be a great story to tell Mr Hughes when, or if, they got back home. The teacher had been explaining to them that the number of funnels corresponded to the ship's power just before they'd slipped away. He'd have to tell Emmie too - so he didn't forget in the meantime. With any luck, the girls would have been able to find their way out of the store cupboard, and Emmie would be waiting for him upstairs.

The Tunnel - Again

Emmie slowly climbed the staircase to B deck, emerging behind the graceful sweep of the banisters which led further upwards. She paused for a moment, conscious that the reception room was busier than she had expected - diners having spilled out of the restaurant with their post-dinner drinks. Pulling out a handkerchief and pretending to dab at her nose gave her an excuse to stop, and she surreptitiously scanned the space, looking for somewhere quiet to sit and wait for Jack.

There seemed to be no options unless she wanted to sit at a table with other people. In her heightened state of anxiety, having checked her watch and seen that just four hours were left, she really didn't want to make small talk. Slowly moving around the room and trying not to draw attention to herself, she noticed an older couple sitting on a sofa in the far corner and looking at her. As she drew nearer, reluctant to change her course so obviously, the man spoke to her. 'Are you looking for somewhere to sit?'

Emmie wasn't sure how to respond, so just nodded back at him.

'We're about to leave,' he said, getting to his feet, 'would you like to sit here?'

'Oh, yes please,' she said, feeling a wave of relief. The change of expression on her face must have been obvious, as the man's wife asked gently if she was alright. 'Yes, thank you - I'm just waiting for someone. He's late.'

This seemed to strike a chord with the woman, who smiled knowingly. 'They always are, my dear.' With this, the couple walked away, causing Emmie to notice that a newspaper had been left on the table beside her. Settling herself down on the sofa, she picked up the paper, unfolded it and began to read. She had angled the paper up so that it largely obscured her torso - hoping that she wouldn't stand out too much in this room of well-to-do passengers.

Over the next quarter of an hour, the room emptied significantly - the diners having finished their drinks, and no doubt heading off to the late evening entertainment. Many people ascended the staircase and were probably destined for the lounge on A deck.

'Drink, madam?' a waiter asked, appearing at her side. 'Oh—' he quickly followed with.

'I'm just waiting for someone,' explained Emmie, lowering the paper slightly.

'Right you are, miss.' The waiter moved away again, stealing a backward glance when he was halfway across the room.

Where was Jack...? Emmie drummed her fingers impatiently on the arm of the sofa. She felt like she was attracting too much attention sat here, but it was the agreed meeting place, so she would just have to wait it out and hope that he didn't take too long.

There were just a handful of passengers still sitting in the reception room when Emmie looked up and saw Jack's head peeking around the corner from the restaurant, having obviously slipped up the stairs directly from the kitchen. He was wearing his blazer again and, amongst these passengers, he blended in fairly well. She dropped the newspaper and raised a hand in greeting.

Grinning, Jack made his way across the room, shooting a sideways look at a couple of men playing cards. They were engrossed in their game and didn't give the tall boy a second thought as he sat down in an armchair next to Emmie's sofa.

'What kept you?' asked Emmie, 'dinner looked like it finished ages ago.' Sighing, Jack recounted the day's events - Emmie's eyes widening as he explained the near miss in the food hoist. 'Did you hurt yourself?' she said, looking concerned.

'No, luckily not,' he replied, 'the hoist slowed down a lot before it got to the bottom of the shaft. It could have been worse.' At this, his voice started to wobble, and it was obvious how scary the experience had really been for Jack. Getting injured in the past would bring even more complexity to their situation.

When he got to the part about dropping the tray of glasses, Emmie put a hand to her mouth, in an attempt to mask a smirk. 'You did what?' she repeated in disbelief. The thought of Jack making such a spectacle in the 1st class dining room was both hilarious and horrifying at the same time.

'How did you and Mary manage to get out of the cupboard, anyway?' asked Jack, switching the conversation topic.

'Ah, well you'd have liked that part for sure,' teased Emmie. 'We had to climb through a ventilation duct and ended up in a linen cupboard.'

'You got Mary to climb through some ducting?' Jack was astonished to hear that the younger girl had been so bold.

'Well, we really didn't have much choice,' Emmie carried on, 'that man was in a real rage, and I wasn't planning on hanging around until he returned.'

Jack nodded in agreement - 'You'd better try and steer clear of him in future too - I get the impression he holds a grudge.'

'I don't think that's going to be too much of a problem,' explained Emmie, and reminded Jack about their deadline for leaving. Lowering her voice and glancing around the room, she added, 'There's less than four hours until the ship sinks - we've got to solve the problem of how to get home.'

'What happened to 'saving Mary'?' Jack asked. 'I thought your time man said that was connected to all of this too?'

'I don't get how it fits together,' Emmie admitted, 'there seems to be something about a rift in time, caused by something we did before and saving Mary is—?'

'Part of fixing it?' suggested Jack. 'Maybe if we know what she needs saving from, then we can save her and fix the rift? That might get us home...'

'You might be right...' Emmie said slowly. 'I can't help thinking that her missing brothers are stopping her being able to do something - maybe looking for them is going to distract her as the ship sinks? 'Saving her' could mean removing that distraction, so she can think clearly.'

'You might be right,' agreed Jack, 'but you haven't been able to find them anywhere - have you?'

Emmie looked down - 'No - not a sign of them,' she said quietly.

Jack then brought out his big concern - 'At what point do we stop trying to solve the time problem, and start thinking about ourselves? If we can't get home, then we're in some serious trouble...' He thought for a moment - 'I like Mary - she seems really nice - but I think we've got to shift focus. And your time man too - how do we know that's even real? We might be putting ourselves at risk for nothing.' He didn't feel good about saying all of this but, having had a lot of time to think whilst stuck in the kitchen, felt they needed to be realistic. Then Jack stood up - 'We should check the tunnel again - we might be able to get the door open now.'

Emmie looked up at him; she didn't like it, but he might be right - they had taken a lot at face value, and the ever-decreasing numbers on her watch were a reminder that they didn't have long left. 'Ok,' she agreed, standing up too, and following him across the room in the direction of the heavy wooden door opposite the stairs.

The room was virtually empty now, so it wasn't difficult to loiter close to the door and quietly slip through when no-one was looking in their direction. As they stepped into the tunnel, their first sensation was the damp, fusty smell of old brickwork and stale air. The door gently shut behind them and their eyes started to adjust to the half-light.

'What are you waiting for? Let's see if we can get out,' Jack said, starting towards the tunnel entrance, which was marked by a thin light filtering around the corner.

'Hold on a second - what was that?' Emmie stood listening hard, one hand cupped around her ear. Her stomach was churning too - the sick feeling she had experienced when they first stepped into the tunnel was back.

'What's what?' replied Jack, earning himself a 'shh' in return.

Suddenly, they heard rushing footsteps, and something collided into them, knocking both friends to the floor. 'Hey, get off!' shouted Jack, finding himself underneath a body with flailing arms and legs. He wriggled his way out, hearing a boy speak with an Irish accent to his side.

'Can you help us? Please!' The boy was almost hysterical - his voice breaking with emotion.

'Patrick? John?' asked Emmie softly, 'is that you?' Immediately, the boy stopped and scrabbled frantically on the floor. 'It's ok,' Emmie continued, 'Mary asked us to help find you.'

'Where's Mary?' came another voice - this one sounding like a slightly younger boy.

'So it is you!' exclaimed Emmie, 'how did you get in here?'

Sniffing, the older boy described how they had been playing hide and seek around the ship and had sneaked through the door, thinking it led to a cupboard or storeroom. 'We were trying to hide from Mary originally - we went into this little room and the floor moved. When the door opened again, she wasn't there.'

'They were in the lift,' Emmie explained to Jack, 'remember I told you Mary had been confused when they disappeared?' Turning back to the boys, she addressed the older one - 'You're Patrick, aren't you? Can you tell us what happened next?'

'Well, we explored some of the ship - it's so grand up here - but then people kept chasing us out of wherever we went, so we decided to find somewhere to hide for a bit.'

John, the younger boy, spoke up again at this point - 'Do you know where Mary is?'

'Yes - she's with your parents,' explained Emmie, 'they've got half the ship's crew looking for you. They're really worried - you've been away since yesterday morning. Why didn't you go back?'

Patrick took up the story again - 'We couldn't. The door we came through shut behind us - we tried knocking on it and shouting, but nothing worked. There's no other way out of this room either.' His voice wavered a little - 'We're really hungry too, and it's cold and damp in here. Can you help us get out?'

'I think so,' replied Emmie, 'the door just opened for us. Your family should be in the general room - let's get you back to them.'

Both boys threw their arms around Emmie at this point, and she could just about see tears on their faces in the dimly lit space.

'You go ahead, and I'll catch you up,' Jack said quietly to Emmie, 'I want to check out the rest of the tunnel.' She understood what Jack wanted to do and headed back towards the door they had just come through.

'Be careful...' she said, gently turning the handle and peering around the door. The room appeared to be empty, and she quickly bundled the grateful brothers out of the tunnel. They headed around the corner towards the restaurant, aiming for the most direct route to the general room.

As the door closed again, Jack suddenly felt very alone and apprehensive about what he might find at the end of the tunnel. There was a lot riding on the rescue of Patrick and John - would that act alone have resolved their own route home?

Pulling himself together, Jack slowly walked towards the distant light filtering in from the tunnel entrance. As he reached the halfway point, he breathed a huge sigh of relief, seeing that the metal wall which had blocked the tunnel had disappeared. A wave of emotion rushed through him, and he found tears of happiness streaming down his cheeks. Picking up his pace, he rounded the corner and could see the mouth of the tunnel. As he got closer, his eyes struggled to see with the light streaming in from outside, and he had to blink a few times to focus properly.

What he then saw made him stop dead in his tracks and put a hand to his mouth in shock. Outside, he had been expecting to see the docks, with his classmates still standing listening to Mr Hughes. Instead, he was greeted with a vast empty, landscape - the featureless ground sloping down to a body of water in the distance. Jack put a hand on the side of the tunnel to steady himself - what was going on? Where was the city, and where was the school party?

He slumped against the wall, feeling totally defeated. They had gone through so much to be able to get back home and, now they could, home seemed to have disappeared. They were caught between two worlds they didn't belong in, and time was running perilously short.

Safe And Sound

Jack turned his head to look at the scene outside the tunnel once again. He still couldn't believe it - where had everything gone?! How could the world they vanish?

He knew that he needed to get back to Emmie - and fast. The conversations about time rifts and saving Mary seemed awfully real now, compared to when he had first heard them. They were going to have to put their heads together like never before, in order to get out of this situation. Then again, argued the other part of his brain, what made him think that they could fix time?

Putting the doubts and worry to one side for a moment, Jack dragged himself away from the tunnel entrance and headed back inside, shoulders slumped and feeling almost resigned to his fate. Literally walking back onto a sinking ship felt ridiculous, yet there seemed no alternative.

As he reached the wooden door back into the ship, the uncertainty returned - this was surely his last chance to pull out. Once he was through that door, it might never open again. His thoughts flicked to Emmie - despite the danger, he couldn't leave her on her own. Mind made up, Jack turned the handle and eased the heavy door open. As it closed behind him with a thud, a group of ladies sitting on the other side of the room looked across to see what was going on. Jack smiled - hoping that this would deflect from what had just happened - and quickly walked over to the restaurant door, before slipping into the darkness inside.

Hurriedly traversing the room, Jack emerged out onto the promenade deck. He could see the lower deck in front of him where they had watched children sliding on the icy surface earlier and headed for the stairs to reach it. Climbing up the other side took him to the entrance to the general room - now to find Emmie...

Pushing the door to the general room open, Jack found that a party was in full swing - there was a piano in the corner being played loudly and a quartet of fiddlers stood gathered around, accompanying the tune. The benches set around the walls were packed with people singing and talking and the middle of the room contained a mass of people dancing. It was very warm inside - at total odds with the freezing conditions on the deck - and the atmosphere was electric.

Jack scanned the room for Emmie, just as another upbeat tune started - the passengers belting out words that they knew well. There were so many figures whirling around that he found it quite disorientating and had to push his way through the crowd. Suddenly, on the other side of the room, he thought he saw Mary and abruptly changed direction to get closer. As the people around him moved and spun, he realised it was definitely Mary, and quickened his pace.

'Mary!' he shouted, closing in on the girl. 'Mary!' She eventually turned around, the music being so loud that speech was almost impossible. Mary smiled at him, and he could see beyond her that Emmie was sat with two young boys and a woman. They must be Patrick and John - it had been hard to make out their features properly in the darkness of the tunnel, but everyone appeared to be really pleased that they were back.

Emmie stood up as she saw Jack approaching and pulled him into the corner, giving him a big hug. 'We did it!' she shouted, close to his ear. He looked back at her, and she knew something was wrong. 'Tell me outside,' she urged, waving to Mary and leading Jack back towards the door.

Once they had got back out into the lobby area, Jack turned to Emmie. 'It's all different,' he said quietly, trying not to cry.

A chill grabbed at Emmie's heart - 'What do you mean? What's different?'

'Everything. The side of the ship had gone, and I looked outside the tunnel but there was nothing there. No docks, no city, no Mr Hughes...'

Emmie looked confused and alarmed at the same time - what on earth was Jack telling her? How could all those things not be there? 'What was outside?' she asked, not sure she wanted to hear the answer.

'Just grass. Flat grass, sloping down to a river or lake. Literally nothing else - not a person or animal in sight.' Jack looked at her, chewing his lip - he was really hoping Emmie had a good suggestion for what to do next. Her face fell - she was experiencing the same crushing disappointment that he had a few minutes previously. They had found the brothers and yet this wasn't enough.

Emmie indicated a bench behind them and suggested they sat down. 'I keep going over what the man told me in my head,' she explained.

'The part about saving Mary?'

'No, not that - something else he said about not removing anything from the ship which belongs here.' Emmie looked at Jack at this point - 'You haven't taken anything, have you?'

'No - of course not. Anyway - like what?'

'Like anything Jack. Come on - this is important!'

Jack racked his brain - he didn't recall taking anything from the ship. In fact, he only had the clothes he was wearing, and they were the same as when the pair arrived. He patted his pockets - nothing. Actually - hold on a minute - what was that...? Pulling out the silver coin he had been given the evening before, he held it up to show Emmie. 'One of the passengers gave me this - could it be what the man meant?'

A strange look passed over Emmie's face - it was relief, mixed with apprehension. 'I'm sure it is - you need to get rid of it. Quickly.' At this point, she checked her watch again and shivered - it showed 3:12 - there were just over three hours to get safely off Titanic, or it would be too late.

'I can't just dump it - it might be valuable,' persisted Jack. 'The man who gave it to me was in 1st class.'

Emmie snorted - 'It won't be much good to us if we drown.' Seeing the shock on Jack's face at this blunt statement, she backtracked slightly - 'Why don't we go back in there and give it to Mary?'

Jack nodded - that was probably the best suggestion in the circumstances. He stood, putting out a hand to pull Emmie up, and together they went back into the general room.

This time, it was easier to spot Mary - she was twirling around in the centre of the room, dancing with one of her brothers. She looked so happy that Jack almost didn't want to disturb her.

'Go on,' insisted Emmie, 'we haven't got time to waste.' She gave him a little push in Mary's direction and smiled at the girl as she noticed them.

'Mary - I, um, found this coin and wanted you to have it. It's American and hopefully will bring you luck in your new life.'

Mary looked at Jack - her eyes welling up a little at this kind act. 'Thank you. It's been a good day - Patrick and John are safe, and this is really nice of you.'

'You're welcome. Maybe see you later?'

As Jack walked back across the room to where Emmie stood, he felt a sense of relief. Even though he hadn't realised accepting the coin might cause a problem, righting the wrong was the best outcome. 'Come on,' he said to Emmie, 'let's hope that was enough.'

*

As the pair left the general room for the second time, they both became aware of a man in a dark overcoat approaching them. He looked cautiously around and then indicated they should move over to the rail at the edge of the deck.

Jack looked questioningly at Emmie - 'It's ok,' she said, 'this is the man I was telling you about.'

'Have you returned the item which belongs on the ship?' the man asked.

'Yes,' Jack confirmed, 'a passenger had given me a coin and I didn't realise it would be a problem to keep it.'

The man nodded - 'That's good - it will help. You have to be very careful with time - it's easy to get things wrong and have an unintended impact.'

'The butterfly effect?' Jack was keen to show that he understood what the man was referring to. 'But what else went wrong? When I looked outside the tunnel, the world was all different.' His face clouded - 'How are we going to get home? *Are* we going to get home?'

The man looked at them in turn - 'I can't be sure. I can only tell you that the time rift will be healed if Mary is saved.'

'What does that mean?' Emmie wanted to know exactly how they needed to help Mary - this wasn't the time for vagaries.

The man's expression was serious now - 'You're on a ship which you know will sink - Mary is meant to survive, but you need to make sure she does. She is supposed to have a big future but, at the moment, it isn't looking good for her.'

'But what about the coin?' Jack asked, 'didn't you say that helped?'

'I did. Your world should be returning to normal now, but the only way to permanently fix time and guarantee you can get home, is to save Mary.'

'Can't we just go back to the tunnel now if the world is fixed?' Jack asked Emmie.

The man answered him - 'The time portal you found in the tunnel isn't there all of the time - it can appear and disappear. All I can tell you is that by saving Mary, you will be able to get home again - even if it appears that you can't.'

'How do we know what you're telling us is right?' Jack demanded. 'You're asking us to take a lot on trust.'

The man stood up - 'You need to hear from your present. Then you'll know it's true.' With that, he walked away, leaving the pair staring at each other.

'What does that mean - 'hear from your present'?' Emmie mused. 'Where on Titanic can you hear from somewhere else?'

Jack scratched his head - 'I don't know... The radio room, perhaps?'

'Good idea - where is it?'

'I don't know, but I'm going to guess that it might be near the bridge - I think we're going to have to go up to the very top deck.'

Emmie looked down at her watch - 2:56 now - they needed to hurry. From what she could remember, the iceberg impact was around two hours before the ship sank - that gave them less than an hour before everything was going to change...

*

Heading down the steps and across the icy deck, Emmie urged Jack to hurry. They clattered up the other side and into the nearest stairwell. Two flights later and the friends emerged on the boat deck.

'The bridge is right at the other end - we need to be quick,' Emmie muttered, pulling her blazer around her to keep out the chill air. The ship was moving quite fast, and a strong wind blew down the length of the deck. They headed into the wind, passing the first group of lifeboats - Emmie shivered at the sight of them, and not just because of the cold.

They passed the giant dome which sat over the main staircase and reached the barrier dividing the officer's promenade from the passenger area. 'We'd better keep close to the side now - don't want to get spotted,' Jack said quietly, as he opened the gate and they slipped through.

Pressed against the ship's superstructure, they edged along, ducking every time there was a window. They came to a door, and Jack peered through the porthole window to see if anyone was on the other side. 'It's clear,' he whispered, slowly turning the handle and easing the door open. Entering, they found themselves in a narrow corridor with various closed doors leading off it. It was quiet - most of the crew being off duty at this late hour.

'Where might the radio room be?' asked Emmie, 'we need to know which way to go.'

'Let's try this way,' murmured Jack, leading them down the corridor to the left. As they reached the end and the corridor ran off in a different direction, Jack raised a finger and stopped. He cupped his hand to his ear - 'Can you hear that?'

'Hear what?' Emmie replied, unsure what she was meant to be listening to.

'That buzzing sound.'

Emmie strained to hear - Jack was right, there was a faint buzzing coming from a door around the corner. It sounded like 'Ber-b-b-b-ber'.

'That's Morse code,' explained Jack, 'it's how Titanic communicated with other ships.'

'But how are we going to hear anything useful from that?'

'I don't know...' admitted Jack, 'this was the most logical place to try though.'

Suddenly, they heard a voice coming from behind the door. Emmie grabbed Jack - 'We should go,' she hissed.

The Argument

'Hold on a minute - listen.' Jack had moved closer to the door to hear better.

'What are you doing?! We need to get out of here before that person comes out.'

Jack didn't move - he had his ear pressed against the door now, much to Emmie's irritation. He beckoned her over and she reluctantly complied. 'Who do you think that sounds like?' he asked.

Emmie's face wore a confused expression - the buzzing noise had stopped and been replaced by a voice which sounded strangely like Mr Hughes. 'How is that happening?' she asked. There was no doubt that it was the teacher's voice now - they could hear him explaining about the number of funnels on Titanic - just as he had been when they slipped away yesterday. Suddenly, a small smile formed on her face - 'I think everything at home is back to normal, after all.'

'Hearing Mr Hughes talking about the funnels just reminded me of something,' Jack replied. 'Apparently, only three of the funnels are actually real - the fourth is just for show, and to vent steam from the kitchen!'

'We'll have to tell him when we get back - I can't wait to see his face,' Emmie couldn't help smiling at this too.

'Just the little matter of getting there now. Come on - let's get out of here. We've just got to make sure Mary gets off the ship safely, then we're done.'

With that, they both looked at each other - realising at the same time that the only way to ensure Mary was safe would be for them to stay on board until the very end... Emmie's face paled, and Jack swallowed nervously - this would be scarier than anything else they had done so far. 'We're literally going to have to wait it out on a sinking ship, aren't we?' whispered Emmie.

Jack nodded slowly, then repeated his suggestion that they leave - holding a hand out to Emmie to emphasise the point. The pair turned and quietly retraced their steps to the outside door. As they closed it behind them, a voice called out - 'What are you doing in here?'

'Quick! Over here,' Jack pulled Emmie across the deck and behind the nearest lifeboat. They could just about crawl along underneath the boat on the very edge of the deck - the keel masking them from view.

'It's high, isn't it...?' said Emmie through gritted teeth. There was just a very thin rail between them and the sea far below. The deck was freezing cold and crawling on their hands and knees was really painful. Once they had passed under the first boat and were able to sit up, they listened to see if anyone was actually following them, rubbing their hands together to warm them up.

'I think we're ok,' muttered Jack, peeking around the end of the lifeboat to check. He stood up and they stepped out from between the boats to carry on back along the deck. 'What's the plan then? Should we find Mary and wait with her to make sure she gets onto a lifeboat?'

'That's probably the best idea,' said Emmie slowly, 'she might wonder why we're hanging around, but I don't suppose there's very long to wait... Let's go and see if she's still at the party?'

'You know - wouldn't we be better off just trying to get out of here?' Jack said abruptly. 'I know that man said we need to save Mary, but so many people are going to die out here tonight - what's the point?'

'No!' snapped Emmie. 'How could you be so selfish?!' Jack stared at her in shock - this was the closest the friends had come to an argument since boarding the ship.

They carried on in silence for a few paces - Emmie's mind whirling frantically. What Jack said was right in a way - how could one small act make so much difference? Then again - the man had been right about everything so far. If they tried to abandon the plan now, there was no guarantee they would actually be able to get home anyway. To top it all off - Mary had become their friend too. What did it make them if they deserted her, knowing there was something that they could have done about it? Finally, she spoke - 'You've seen first-hand what it's like when the world we know changes - doesn't the possibility of that being permanent frighten you?'

Now it was Jack's turn to be lost for words - he mulled over the feeling of absolute despair which had struck him on finding that the tunnel didn't lead back to home as he remembered it. That was as low a point as he could ever remember - everything he knew swept away in an instant. 'But... we could die trying—' he eventually managed.

'Yes - or we could get stuck in 1912 permanently,' Emmie shot back. 'The only thing we've got to go on is what the man told us - he was spot on about everything else. He also suggested that we somehow caused this time rift in the first place - don't you feel responsible for sorting that out?'

'I guess...' conceded Jack, though he wasn't really sure - self-preservation had kicked in, and he was struggling to think about the needs of others.

They reached the end of the deck without completely agreeing on a way forward, then climbed down the stairs and out onto the larger deck area in front of the general room. There were still lights on but, when they reached the room, they could see the party was over and very few people remained. Emmie's eyes narrowed - there was a familiar figure sitting on one of the benches at the back of the room. 'Come on,' she said to Jack, 'we need to get this straight once and for all.'

As Emmie led the way into the general room, Jack recognised the man in the dark overcoat and groaned inwardly. He could see where this was going. The man looked up as they approached - 'Did you hear what you needed to hear?'

'Yes, thank you,' answered Emmie. 'We do need to know though - what's so special about Mary?'

The man looked at her - 'Are you working out whether to stay and help or not?'

Emmie flushed - was it that obvious? 'It's such a big thing,' she admitted, 'we think our world - the future - is back to normal. Staying is just a massive risk.'

'I can't tell you exactly why Mary is special,' said the man gently, 'other than that she becomes part of a discovery which had a big impact on the outcome of the Second World War.'

Emmie and Jack looked at each other - this made more sense now. If there was a risk that the outcome of the war could be different, then their world could change dramatically once again.

'I didn't tell you this before,' said the man, 'but it might help. The reason this time rift happened was because one of you returned home before with something from 1940.'

Suddenly, Jack knew exactly what had happened. 'The penny!' he gasped, raising a hand to his mouth in horror. When they had escaped from the Blitz, he had discovered a one pence coin in his pocket - left over from the meal they had bought on the last day. He had totally forgotten about the coin until now... 'We'll help,' he said quickly, 'it's my fault - I need to put it right.'

The man smiled at him - 'It will be ok in the end,' he promised, 'even if it doesn't look like it. Good luck.' With that, he rose and left the room, turning and touching his finger to his hat on the way out.

Jack turned to Emmie - 'Do you know where Mary's cabin is?' he asked.

'Yes - it's near the back, on F deck,' she replied, leading the way out of the general room. They descended three flights of stairs, down to the Kelly's cabin. It was a strange feeling - knowing that something terrible was about to happen, which you couldn't do anything about, yet had to stay and witness.

As they reached the bottom of the steps, Emmie quickened her pace and disappeared around a corner, into a group of passengers. 'Mary!' she called, thinking she had seen the girl up ahead. The figure she was hailing turned around and Emmie called again - 'Oh Mary - it's you.'

'Of course it's me,' replied Mary in confusion, and Emmie saw that she was with a tall man that she took to be her father. They were just opening the door to a cabin as she had called to Mary.

'Father - this is Emmie. She helped to find Patrick and John. She was the one who brought them up to the party earlier.'

'Thank you for your help, Emmie,' said John Kelly, offering his hand to her, as Jack caught the group up too. 'I was talking to the purser when you brought the boys back - we're so very grateful.' His brow furrowed and he continued - 'The one thing I don't understand though is where you found them. They told me they'd got stuck in a tunnel...?'

'Well—' began Emmie, but that was as far as she got, as a sudden shudder rippled across the floor, growing in intensity. The vibration was matched by a tearing noise which sounded like a piece of material being ripped in two. Those who were standing grabbed onto the walls for support, and Emmie could see that inside the cabin a glass had slipped off the washstand and smashed on the floor. There was a moment of pure silence after the ripping sound, and then everyone started talking at once - cabin doors flew open, and people stumbled out into the passage in their nightwear. There were a few screams at the shock of what had happened, but most of the passengers seemed more bemused than anything.

Jack looked at Emmie - his eyes wide with fear. 'It's happening, isn't it?' he asked quietly, trying to hold back his tears.

'Don't panic everyone, I'm sure it's nothing to worry about,' John Kelly said reassuringly. 'I'll head forward and see what I can find out.'

'No, Father. Please can we stay together?' begged Mary, but it was too late - he was already halfway down the corridor and disappearing around the corner, even as she spoke.

How Bad Is It?

'Look - the floor is sloping! What do you think is going on?' Mary turned to Emmie and Jack, wide-eyed and panicked. The floor, which had previously had a slight tilt to the left, had now definitely shifted to the right - the overall change being very noticeable.

Jack and Emmie looked at each other - neither knowing what to say. If this was the iceberg strike - and it seemed certain that it was - then it was only a matter of time before everyone on board knew about it anyway. Still, admitting it out loud would make it feel more real than they wanted to admit to themselves.

'I don't know... Maybe one of the engines had a problem?' Jack attempted a plausible explanation, but he was far from convinced by himself.

'Listen though - you can still hear them...' Mary said, straining to concentrate over the nervous chatter from all around them. 'I'm going to follow Father - see what's happening.'

'Wait up,' Emmie called, giving Jack's arm a tug. He pulled a face at her but let himself be steered along the corridor. As they quickly walked around the corner to the stairs, Jack turned to Emmie.

'Are you sure about this? It's Mary we really need to save,' he whispered. Mary was a few paces in front and took the stairs two at a time - they had never seen the younger girl so determined. Up she went, leading them to the wide service corridor on E deck.

'And you think she'll get on a lifeboat without her dad?' asked Emmie scornfully.

'I guess we're heading in the right direction at least,' muttered Jack, more to cheer himself up than anything.

As the pair hurried after Mary, Emmie noticed that those crew members who she saw looked quite worried. They obviously knew that something was up but were trying to keep the passengers from panicking. Turning a corner, they saw a crewman with a wrench by one of the heavy steel doors dividing the corridor.

'Those are watertight doors,' cried Jack, 'he's getting ready to close them.' The man ignored him as they passed through the doorway and carried on winding a large nut on the door with the wrench. Jack turned to look behind him and saw the door sliding closed. There was a heavy metal clang, and his heart felt like it had dropped to the floor. 'It must be sinking!' he shouted, losing all sense of subtlety in his panic.

Emmie and Mary both stopped and stared - horrified for different, yet similar, reasons. 'Come on,' Emmie said to Jack, walking over and taking his arm, 'we need to hold this together. Look - no-one else is getting flustered.' This was largely true - although the crew appeared concerned, everyone was calmly going about their jobs still.

'Don't worry, laddie,' came a gruff voice from behind them, 'this ship is unsinkable - didn't you read the posters?' Jack looked up and saw a small, grizzled sailor in a stained white jacket. The dough stains on the front marked him out as a baker, and Jack wasn't sure whether he was being serious or not. He nodded and smiled thinly at the man. 'Why don't you go back to your cabin and get some rest?' the baker suggested.

'We're just looking for my father - he went to see what was happening,' Mary explained quietly.

'Well, I'm sure he'll be back soon - there are stairs at the end, you can use those if you need to.' With that, the man disappeared into one of the many crew cabins along the corridor, leaving the group to ponder their next move.

'I'm sure Father would have come through here.' Mary was looking back along the route they had walked, trying to see if there was anywhere that he might have stopped to investigate.

'The noise seemed to come from the front of the ship,' suggested Emmie, 'should we go further forward and see if we can find him up there?' Mary nodded in agreement, and they set off once again. Fairly soon, they passed the cupboard which Mary and Emmie had been locked in, and both girls let out an involuntary shiver. Hurrying past, they came to two sets of stairs, leading both up and down.

'Which ones?' asked Jack.

'Let's go with the second set - they're further forward,' Mary decided, rounding the corner of the stairwell and starting the descent. There was a steady stream of people coming up the other way and they had to squeeze into the side in order to pass. It was a strange sight - some passengers were in just their nightwear, seemingly trying to find out what was going on, whilst others were fully dressed, and hugging possessions close to them.

'This is getting chaotic,' murmured Emmie, 'something must be up.' They got their answer after trying to descend by a further deck. As they turned into the stairwell, the sound of rushing water reached their ears.

Looking down the steps, Jack stopped in a mixture of amazement and shock. 'The whole corridor is flooded!' he said, his voice rising an octave or two. Emmie and Mary peered over his shoulder and confirmed this for themselves.

'H... how did that happen...?' stammered Mary, 'I thought that was what the watertight doors were for?'

'I think the ship must have hit something, and that's what has caused the water to flood in,' said Emmie carefully. She was trying to control her breathing, in order to stem the rising panic in her chest. Aside of the impact, this was the first time they had been confronted with the reality of what was about to happen to Titanic. 'I'm sure the watertight doors will stop the water flooding any further.'

'But it's going to come up the stairs, isn't it? There's no door on them...' Mary appeared to have made a critical deduction the designers may not have considered.

Emmie looked at the girl and decided to level with her - well, as much as she felt she could get away with anyway. 'I think you're right,' she said, 'we have no way of knowing where the water is coming from, or how fast it is coming in, but if that deck fills up then it's going to come up the stairs.'

'And maybe the next ones after that too?' Mary asked.

'It's possible, yes. That's why we should focus on finding your father and getting you back to your family.'

Jack joined in now - 'Where do you think he would have gone - it doesn't look like he's down here?'

'I think we should go back up - there were more cabins on the deck above. He might have been looking for someone he knew to ask what was going on.' Mary was trying to get inside her father's mind, but it wasn't easy. 'If not, he'll probably have gone to find the purser - he would know what was happening. His office is on E deck - we almost walked past it earlier.'

Emmie was frowning - 'How are we going to get past those watertight doors though? They'll stop us going back the way we came.'

'Just go up another level,' suggested Jack. 'Unless the doors are on every deck?'

'Genius!' replied Emmie - sometimes Jack threw in the greatest suggestions.

Buoyed by his proposal, Jack led the way back along the corridor and up the small staircase into the kitchens. It seemed like a lifetime ago that he had run from whoever shouted at him on the same steps that morning.

As they ran through the kitchen and out into the dining room beyond, Mary tripped over a chair leg, falling with a cry to the ground. 'Aargh!'

'Are you alright?' asked Emmie, skidding to a halt and going back over to the girl.

Mary wriggled her foot - 'I think so. It just stings a bit.' She got to her feet gingerly - 'Where do we go from here? I just want to find my father.'

'Well,' said Jack, 'just through there...' he pointed to the double doors at the end of the room, 'there's some steps going down. I'm fairly sure they come out somewhere near the purser's desk.'

'Oh good,' said Mary gratefully. 'Hopefully Father will be there.'

*

Hurrying down the staircase towards E deck and the purser's desk, there were a steady stream of people passing them - both passengers and crew. Like earlier, the passengers were a curious mix of some in their nightwear, looking like they had just been awakened, and others fully dressed. As they reached the landing ahead of E deck, their descent came to an abrupt halt, with a queue of people spilling back up the stairs.

Emmie craned her neck to get a better look and could see that there was a large crowd gathered in front of the steps. She wondered what was going on - the purser's desk was just around the corner and this crowd was right in the way.

'Listen up! Listen up!' came an authoritative voice from somewhere in the crowd, and everyone fell silent. 'The ship has hit an iceberg and sustained some minor damage. There is no need to panic—' At this, everyone began talking at once, and the speaker had to shout for calm. 'I repeat, there is no need to panic. If it becomes necessary to take to the lifeboats, then the crew will inform you at the right time.'

'There's Father!' shouted Mary, squeezing between the people standing in front of them and trying to push her way through the crowd. Emmie and Jack looked at one another and followed.

'Let's just make sure they're all together,' suggested Emmie, 'then we'll get out of here.'

'If we still can,' added Jack gloomily. Now the crew appeared to be acknowledging the severity of the situation, he was feeling far from happy about still being on board.

Edging their way through the crowd, Emmie could still just about see Mary in front of them. She was ploughing on relentlessly, stubbornly refusing to let anything or anyone get in the way of her reaching her father.

'Father!' she heard Mary call out, and saw Mr Kelly appear from behind another man - turning his head in surprise to look at her.

'Mary! What are you doing up here?'

'I followed when you went off to see what had happened to the ship. I called after you as I didn't want to lose you, but you didn't hear me.' Mary's words were tumbling out now as her father put his arm around her and held on tight.

'It doesn't sound good,' he admitted to her, 'and I'm not quite sure how to get back down to your mother with all of these watertight doors shut.'

'Emmie and Jack can help us with that - they're just behind me. Emmie knows her way around really well,' said Mary proudly.

'It sounds like I may have to thank you again,' John Kelly acknowledged, as he saw Emmie and Jack making their way through the emptying room. 'Mary tells me that you can help us find our way downstairs again?'

Emmie looked at him nervously - keen to help the family to safety as soon as possible, so that she could focus on their own plight. 'I can certainly try.' She pointed back at the stairs - 'We need to go back up again as there are no watertight doors on that deck. Then we can cut through and get to the stairs nearest your cabin.'

'What are we waiting for then?' John Kelly led them towards the stairs, following Emmie's instructions. As they walked towards the 3rd class stairs, they passed numerous passengers talking in little huddled groups. It was hard to hear what was being said, but the sentiment was all too clear - everyone was feeling quite scared. Although Titanic was described as unsinkable, the mention of lifeboats had spooked all that had heard it.

At the top of the stairs, several stewards were lined up between the 2nd class corridor which the group were walking along, and the stairs themselves. They were facing the stairs and enforcing the segregation between the different classes of passenger.

'May we pass?' John Kelly asked politely, 'I've just been to see the purser.' The nearest steward stood aside to let them past, moving back into line when they had done so. Turning back to the man, Mr Kelly continued - 'What is your purpose?'

The steward looked uncertain for a moment, before replying - 'All passengers need to remain in their respective areas of the ship whilst the captain assesses the damage.'

'Very well,' he said and motioned to the others to follow him down the stairs. As they reached the bottom and turned towards the Kelly's cabin, they ran into a small crowd of people who had gathered in the corridor.

'I heard this deck's already underwater at the front of the ship,' said one man.

'And they're not letting anyone up to the lifeboats,' another joined in. 'If you ask me - we've had it...'

Before long, the mood had deteriorated - many of the passengers were crying and tempers were beginning to fray. A couple of men came down the stairs, muttering angrily about the stewards segregating the classes. 'It's wrong,' said one of them, 'keeping us down here until everyone else is alright.'

'We need to keep calm - they'll send people to the boats when it's the right time.' John Kelly pushed his way into the crowd and spoke confidently. 'I've just been up to the purser - they're looking at the damage and will then decide what to do.'

This seemed to settle the crowd a little - one of their own was talking and, for that reason alone, he commanded more respect and credibility than any anonymous crew member.

Just as John Kelly had finished speaking, there was a commotion from the stairwell and a man burst into the corridor, red-faced and with sweat running down his face. 'The water's up to the deck above!' he shouted. 'The ship's going down fast!'

We're Going To Be Ok

There was immediate alarm amongst the assembled passengers. John Kelly's calming words of a few moments ago were forgotten in an instant, as survival mode kicked in. So many conversations were happening at once in a confined space, that people had resorted to almost shouting to each other. When you added in the wailing and general background noise, it all added up to an impossible situation.

'*CALM*, everyone, calm!' Mary's father shouted, in an attempt to make himself heard. He was an intelligent man and could see the situation might easily get out of control. As the noise subsided a little, he motioned to the deck above - 'How do you know the water is above us?' he asked, searching the crowd for the man who had spoken previously. 'Surely the watertight doors mean you can't get forward on the deck above?'

A silence descended as the crowd realised that this was an important question, then there was a momentary pause before they received their answer. 'The doors are open again,' said a voice belonging to the man who had come down the stairs in such a hurry. 'I heard one of the crew saying they needed to open them to level out the flooding.'

This last statement brought further panic amongst the passengers, many of whom couldn't swim, and multiple conversations started up again - each person trying to talk over the others. Mary stared at her father - willing him to say the right words again to soothe the agitated folk all around her. Jack nudged Emmie at this point, gesturing that they should leave.

'We can't go now - we need to make sure Mary and her family get to safety,' Emmie whispered.

Jack stood chewing his lip, his face close to tears. He wanted to help, but the thought of drowning or freezing to death was really scary. 'How long have we got left?' he muttered to Emmie.

She looked at the watch on her wrist - hurriedly pulling her sleeve back down afterwards, as if that act alone could shield them from time itself. 'Just under two hours,' she sniffed. It wasn't long.

*

'What did you actually see?' Emmie turned back into the crowd as Mr Kelly started to speak again.

'Well... I was going forward to find out what was happening,' began the man, as their fellow passengers stopped and listened once more. 'I could tell that the ship was starting to dip forward, so I wanted to see for myself.' He paused for a moment, unsure quite how much to say, for fear of doing more harm than good.

'Go on...' John Kelly's stare loosened the man's tongue once more.

'So, I got to the end of that wide corridor - 'Scotland Road' I think the crew call it - and there are some steps which take you down to the single men's cabins. I went down, and there was water all over the floor - sloshing around it was. I must have been on the stairs about a minute, and I swear I saw it rise by one step in just that time.'

'Thought you came down here saying it was on the deck above...?' shouted a man with a grey cloth cap further back in the crowd. 'Which is it?' There were additional murmurs of dissent coming from all corners now - none of the passengers really wanted to believe that there was anything wrong with the unsinkable ship.

'I came back up the stairs,' the man continued, 'and went a bit further forward - the mail room must be under where I was, as there were loads of mail sacks which had been dragged up and left at the top of the stairs. Anyway, the water was all the way up those forward stairs and lapping at the sacks.'

'So, we're nose heavy and taking on water, it seems,' concluded John Kelly. 'Did you talk to any of the crew? Did they say anything useful?'

'There were quite a lot of people about, especially down at the front. Most of them were trying to move things so they didn't get wet - like the sacks of mail.' The man paused for a minute, looking nervously around the crowd - he wasn't used to speaking to so many people at once. 'The ones I did ask told me not to worry. They said it was all under control, and that there was a plan to even out the flooding - that's when the doors were mentioned.'

'Did you see anyone going up to the lifeboats?' a woman next to Emmie asked. 'That would show how confident they were about their plan?'

'There's a queue at the bottom of the 2nd class staircase,' replied the man, 'I had a look through the doors from the corridor. Don't know what they're queuing for, but everyone looked warmly dressed.'

The talking started once more - little conversations everywhere, pushing the volume in the narrow corridor up and making it hard to think. There were mutters of 'No problem then' and 'I don't want to take my chances in a lifeboat,' as the initial panic from the crowd gave way to an uneasy indifference. John Kelly looked a lot more relaxed as well - the assessment not having been as bad as he must have feared.

Emmie took Jack's arm and led him slightly further back from the assembled group. 'We need to warn them that this is real,' she said quietly, 'if they stay down here and refuse to go for the lifeboats then lots of them will drown.'

'You heard what the man said earlier though - we need make sure Mary's ok, but we've done enough damage without realising it already,' reasoned Jack, 'I don't dare make it any worse...'

Emmie looked uncomfortable, as though she was wrestling with her conscience. 'Agreed, but that doesn't stop it hurting. What a horrible set of options...' She sniffed and looked down at her feet - the answer wasn't down there, but it didn't seem like it was anywhere else either. 'I guess we can't alter the fact that there aren't enough lifeboats,' she dropped her voice even further for fear of being overheard. 'We can't alter the fact that there will be selfish people and selfless people, and we can't alter the fact that a lot of people on this ship will be dead in a few hours—' Emmie stopped at this point - choking back a rush of sadness which threatened to overwhelm her emotions. 'We have to focus on what we can do - and that's helping Mary and her family. We need to make sure they get upstairs and into a lifeboat before it's too late.'

Jack's mouth gaped - he'd never heard his friend speak so passionately on a subject before. She was right too - it was an awful situation, choosing to ignore the chance to help real people who were stood in front of them. It was for the greater good - which sounded fine until you were actually faced with the reality of it. 'What do you think we should do next?' he asked.

'I say we go and see for ourselves what's happening - maybe we can come back and talk quietly to Mary's dad?'

'Ok, but how about we take Mary and her dad with us - they can see for themselves then?'

*

And so it was - a few minutes later the four of them, led by John Kelly, emerged from the stairs and started along the wide corridor which they had learned was called Scotland Road. It was named after a street in Liverpool, where many of the ship's crew were from. Mary held her father's hand, and Jack walked alongside Emmie, just behind.

'What do you think we're going to find?' asked Mr Kelly. He was curious to see the damage for himself but was a lot less worried than when the man had first burst in, shouting about flooding.

'Hopefully we'll be able to see how bad it is for ourselves, and maybe even find someone in charge who can tell us what the plan is,' said Jack hopefully. In truth, a small part of him wanted to see what destruction lay at the front end of the ship too.

Mary jumped as they passed the entrance to the engine room and the door sprung open, two men covered in greasy overalls appearing. 'Mind out!' they shouted, as they charged off down the corridor, leaving the door swinging behind them.

'Wonder what that's about?' said Jack, surprised by their sudden appearance too. They got their answer a moment or two later as the men returned, dragging a large length of rubber pipe with them. 'Maybe they're trying to pump some of the water out?' he suggested.

At the end of the corridor, near where the pile of mail sacks had apparently been seen, Emmie noticed a hunched figure sitting on a wooden chest. He was dressed in black and, as she looked, a trickle of water emerged from around the corner and started to lap at his feet. The man didn't seem to notice and continued to stare into the distance.

Quickly realising it was the time architect, Emmie called to the man - 'Hello! Are you alright?' As he turned to look at them, she gave him a wink and asked again - 'Are you alright?'

The man eventually spoke - 'What are you doing down here? I'd get out and save yourselves while you can,' he said miserably, showing no sign of recognising Emmie or Jack.

John Kelly crouched down next to the man - 'If it's so bad, why are you still down here?'

'What's the point? The ship's doomed and we're not all going to get off. There aren't enough lifeboats—'

'What?! How would you know a thing like that?' He turned to look back at Mary, Emmie and Jack before continuing, 'Are you part of the crew?'

The man paused for a moment, and Emmie was convinced he was quickly fabricating a story. He then spoke again - 'I work for Cunard - we make the fastest liners in the world, but Titanic is so much bigger than anything else afloat that we needed to know how it was done.' He stopped, apparently surprised at his own outburst.

'Go on,' Mr Kelly said, in a gentle but firm voice.

'My job was to take a trip on Titanic and report back. I've spent the voyage so far looking at how everything works.'

'And taking notes too?' added Jack, catching on to the need for realism.

The man nodded - 'Not a lot of good it'll do now though...'

Suddenly, Emmie had an idea - 'How much do you really know about the danger we're in?' she asked.

Clearing his throat, the man spoke again - 'Titanic was built with a number of watertight compartments - she can stay afloat with up to four of these being breached - but I strongly suspect more have been damaged. The ship hit an iceberg, you see, and it appears to have torn a gash in the side - a long gash.' He stopped, aware of the horrified looks on the faces staring at him, as the details hit them. 'It's worse,' he continued, 'there are only twenty lifeboats up there, each able to carry around sixty people. There are over two thousand passengers and crew - you do the calculations...'

'Why are there so few lifeboats?' Emmie said, 'isn't that quite short-sighted?'

'We believe it was a design decision,' explained the man, 'there were plans for more, but Titanic was built to be the most luxurious liner afloat, and the designers didn't want lifeboats getting in the way of the view from cabins they could sell for a lot of money.' His face fell in mock horror at revealing the big secret.

'Would you come and talk to the passengers who are still down below?' asked Mr Kelly, after a pause. 'They're not taking the danger seriously, and most of them don't believe there is a need to use the lifeboats. I'm worried that they will get left behind if we don't do something.'

'I don't see what I can do - why would they listen to me? I'm just a nobody to them.'

'Please?' John Kelly's request now carried just the tiniest bit of a demand within it. 'You know what you're talking about - that's what they need to hear. You've spent a couple of minutes explaining everything to us, and now we're convinced.'

The man shrugged and slowly got to his feet - 'Ok then, if you think it'll help...'

Suddenly, a dull thud could be heard from somewhere beneath them, the noise reverberating around the decks below. Immediately, the floor, which had been sloping to the right, lurched in the other direction, throwing them all off balance. Jack grabbed onto Emmie, who in turn reached out for Mary. Mr Kelly's face turned white as a sheet, as he braced himself against the corridor wall, trying to stay upright. 'Come on man! Quickly!' he shouted.

Time To Leave

Back at the foot of the F deck stairwell, the crowd from earlier had largely dispersed - people having either gone back to their cabins or, in a few cases, ventured up to the top of the stairs to see what was going on.

Jack whispered to Emmie - 'Does this count as messing about with the time rules?' He felt uneasy with what they were doing, even if it would help Mary's family.

'I'm hoping it's ok, as Mary's father decided to do it - not us.' She turned to Mr Kelly - 'Do you think this is going to be a waste of time if everyone's gone?'

'Don't you worry about that,' he replied, walking up and down the corridor, knocking on doors as he went. There was a fair amount of grumbling, and a few doors were opened, then abruptly shut in his face, but after about ten minutes, a reasonable crowd had gathered once more. The Kelly family were all lined up beside their father - proud that he was trying to do the right thing. Bridget Kelly was holding tight to her husband's hand, having been really worried when he took it upon himself to find out what was going on.

It became obvious to Emmie that not all of the people present were from English-speaking countries, and she was concerned about how much of the warning they might understand. Walking over to a group of passengers who appeared to be Scandinavian, she asked if any of them spoke English. One man shyly put up his hand. 'Excellent!' exclaimed Emmie, 'will you translate back to the others for me please?'

'Yes, no problem,' replied the man. 'What are you going to tell us?'

'Not me - him,' Emmie explained, pointing to the time architect. 'Please listen carefully - it's important.' She walked back through the crowd, nodding to Mr Kelly, who then indicated that the man should speak.

He cleared his throat, his story coming out easily the second time - 'I work for Cunard - another shipping company - so I know a few things about these liners. I'm afraid the damage to Titanic is bad - there's flooding at the front and too many of the watertight compartments have been breached for her to stay afloat.'

The group of passengers were eerily silent. Pausing for a moment, he looked around for a reaction, but there was none - just a sea of shocked faces staring back at him.

After what seemed like an eternity, a woman spoke - 'Do you mean the ship's going to sink?'

'I'm afraid so. You can probably tell that the floor is sloping forwards a little - that's because the water rushing in is pulling the front part of the ship down. The further down it goes, the more water comes in.'

The reaction came all of a sudden - people talking over each other and shouting questions at the man. There were a lot of tears too - the shock breaking out in a savage rush of emotion.

'Listen up!' John Kelly said, waving his arms at the front of the assembled passengers. 'Listen up and he'll tell you what to do.'

The volume dipped again, though not to the low level of before, compelling the man to almost shout his instructions. 'You have to get to the lifeboat deck,' he explained, 'they'll probably board women and children first, but you need to get up there quickly.' He had decided against mentioning that there weren't enough lifeboats, so as not to cause panic. No-one could do anything about the lack of capacity - their best chance was to be in the right place at the right time.

The crowd began to disperse - some people heading straight for the stairs, whilst others quickly retrieved coats and armfuls of possessions from their cabins. His work done, the man sank down beside the stairs and put his head in his hands once more.

'Don't give up now,' John Kelly told him, reaching down and taking the man by his hand. He hauled him to his feet and continued - 'You've done a great thing tonight - most of these passengers would have sat it out down here and not understood the danger. You've given them a chance.' He held out his hand again, and the man shook it.

'Don't leave it too late yourself,' he instructed, 'looks like you've got a family to take care of.' He nodded to Bridget, then gave Emmie a meaningful look, before turning and striding up the staircase.

'He's right,' Mary's father said, 'we need to go now too.'

'Are you coming with us?' Mary asked Jack and Emmie.

'No - we really better get back upstairs and find the steward who is chaperoning me,' said Emmie. She was relieved the family were heading to safety but realised that every minute her and Jack spent on the ship increased the risk of them not being able to get home.

Mary sniffed, and two large tears rolled down her cheeks - 'Will you be alright?' she asked quietly.

'Oh yes, we'll be fine - don't worry about us,' Emmie reassured her. She reached out to hug the girl, who held her tightly. As she pulled away, Mary hugged Jack too - 'Thank you both so much for helping us,' she said, blinking the tears away. 'I'll always be grateful to you for finding Patrick and John,' then, lowering her voice, she added - 'and it was great fun exploring the parts of the ship we weren't meant to.'

Jack, who had gone unusually quiet at this point, eventually found some words and managed to wish them well. Goodbyes said, John Kelly led his family up the stairs, turning and thanking them sincerely for their help before he disappeared from sight.

*

'Just us now...' Jack said quietly, in the empty corridor. The ship was making strange creaking noises and he was feeling very unnerved by them. 'Is it finally time to go?'

'Yes, I think it is - we've done all we can now. Just need to get back into the tunnel before it's too late.' Emmie looked around - 'What's the best way for us to get there quickly?'

'I reckon it's got to be that staircase from the kitchen.' Jack was right - there would be people everywhere on the decks above and the service stairs would hopefully let them avoid the congestion. He led the way back up to D deck, glad to see that the stewards who had been stood at the top of the stairs had disappeared. The pair ran through the 2nd class dining room and into the kitchen corridor - Emmie thinking how long ago it seemed that she had opened this very door looking for Jack, yet it was only yesterday.

As they clattered into the main kitchen, Jack stopped as he saw a figure in the corner, seemingly scooping something into a bag. Emmie gave him a shove - 'Forget him - no time to stop now!' and led the way quickly up the spiral stairs in the semi-darkness. At one point, she stopped to listen as it sounded like someone was coming down, causing Jack to walk straight into the back of her.

'Oof,' she grunted, 'be careful - you don't want to fall back down!'

'Don't stop then,' he grumbled, as Emmie started to climb once more.

Emerging at the top into the small restaurant kitchen, Jack grabbed Emmie's hand and pulled her through the open doorway and into the restaurant itself. The room was brightly lit, despite being empty, and gave the impression of a space which had been vacated in a hurry. They walked quickly across the thick carpet; past chairs left out untidily from their tables.

As they reached the door, Emmie put her finger to her lips and leaned in close to listen. 'There are people out there talking,' she whispered.

'What are we going to do?' asked Jack.

'Not a lot we can do - we need to get out there before it's too late.'

Jack gulped a little - he didn't want to get all this way and then get into trouble with one of the crew members again. 'Ok...' he said warily.

Emmie put her hand on the door handle and gently turned it. It swung open, revealing an empty corridor leading onto the main reception space they were headed for. There were definitely voices coming from beyond though - and it sounded like quite a lot of them. 'Come on,' Emmie took Jack's hand and they edged along the corridor, stopping at the end to peer around the corner.

The sight that greeted them was not what they were expecting - there was a queue of well-dressed passengers snaking along one of the forward corridors, and up the grand staircase in the centre of the room. For such a dangerously balanced situation, the passengers were behaving in a very orderly way.

'I don't think they'll see us if we're quick,' reasoned Jack - the queue was coming into the room on the far side, and no-one seemed to be paying any attention to the restaurant entrance. The heavy curtain which had partially hung over the door the day before was still there, and it wouldn't take many paces to cover the distance to it.

'Let's chance it,' agreed Emmie. 'Ready?'

'Ready,' nodded Jack, and the pair quickly strode over to the door, slipping behind the curtain as they reached it. They both breathed a sigh of relief, hearts still pounding at the thought of being challenged. Jack felt behind him for the handle, patting along the wooden door until he touched it. 'Say goodbye to Titanic,' he said, turning the handle.

Nothing happened. The catch rattled, but the door didn't open. Trying again, Jack turned around to look closer, his concern about being spotted evaporating as the fear of being stuck rose in his chest.

'What's going on?' asked Emmie. 'Is it stiff?'

'No,' replied Jack, his face pale against the dark wood of the door, 'it's locked. We're stuck...'

Trapped

'Locked?' Emmie said, 'what do you mean - locked?'

'I mean the door's locked, and it won't open,' Jack replied, his voice dulled with disappointment.

'Let me have a go.' Emmie wriggled past Jack and tried the handle. The door rattled but didn't budge. She tried it again - this time working the arm up and down rapidly but, aside of making a fair bit of noise, nothing happened. Her face fell and she gave an angry sigh - everything they'd been through, and now it all came down to a locked door...

'We should have come up earlier,' muttered Jack, looking at the floor. His previous enthusiasm had drained away, and he was fighting himself to retain some perspective. 'We're stuck on this ship now... Except we're not, because if we stay then we're going to drown...'

Emmie turned to look at him - her eyes were welling up and she was just as distraught as he was. She knew it had been her idea to stay and help Mary's family out - it had been the right thing to do, but now she wondered what the cost to them would be.

'Could we break the door down?' suggested Jack, but then remembered the queue of people on the other side of the room. It was quite a surprise that no-one appeared to have heard their attempts to open the door so far.

'I guess it's worth a try,' said Emmie grimly, 'we'll need something quite heavy though - the door is really thick.'

Jack looked around, settling on a chair close by - it looked sturdy, and might be enough to force their way through. He picked it up, working out how best to breach the door.

Some angry shouting broke out on the deck above, drifting down the staircase. 'Do it now!' said Emmie urgently - hoping that the noise might be masked by the sudden commotion.

Jack lifted the chair and attempted to swing it at the door. It was much heavier that he had expected, and he only managed to leave a scratch on the surface.

'Give me a hand?' he asked, furtively looking around to see if they had been noticed.

Emmie picked up the chair with Jack for a second attempt, and together they ran at the door, landing a heavy blow from all four legs at the same time. The bang reverberated around the room, but the door stood solid.

'What's going on over there?!' shouted a voice. Jack looked around to see a steward at the top of the stairs - he was glaring angrily in their direction and, worse still, the queuing passengers were now looking at them too. 'Come on - we need to get out of here before he comes down,' Jack said, grabbing Emmie by the hand.

Running across the room to further shouts from the staircase, they headed down a corridor on the opposite side of the ship from the queue. They slowed to a normal pace as they walked past rows of cabin doors, to avoid drawing more attention to themselves.

'Well, what are we going to do now then?' demanded Jack. He was really rattled and struggling to think straight.

'We're going to have to join a queue and take our chances in one of the lifeboats,' Emmie replied quietly.

'Probably not that queue though - we best head for the next staircase.'

'But how does that help us get home?'

'I don't know if it does, but I'd rather be alive and stuck in 1912 than the alternative...'

Jack looked across at her, unsure what to say. He trusted Emmie's judgement, but this was a big predicament to get out of. Living permanently in 1912 wasn't at all attractive, even assuming they made it to a lifeboat and safety.

'Come on,' she encouraged, 'not a lot of other options really, are there?'

A door opened ahead of them, and Jack quickly pulled Emmie into the nearest cabin doorway. The door itself was shut, but it was set back slightly from the corridor so there was room for them to stand out of view. Listening, they heard some people emerge up ahead, talking to each other, 'Quickly dear, you don't need all that - just your warm coat.'

Emmie shivered a little in their hiding place - it was going to be really cold outside, and they were both in just their school blazers still. Looking behind her, she reached for the doorknob and turned it - the door silently swinging open.

'What are you doing?!' hissed Jack, 'we need to get out!'

'Wait here,' said Emmie, slipping into the darkened room.

Jack turned around and poked his head back out into the corridor to check no-one was coming. They couldn't afford any more delays if they were to get off the ship in time.

'These will keep us warm,' announced Emmie, emerging with two tartan blankets in her hand. 'It's going to be freezing out on the deck, let alone in a lifeboat for who knows how long...'

Jack took a blanket gratefully and hung it over his arm. 'Thanks.' Looking out again, he saw that the corridor was still empty - the departing passengers long gone. 'All clear,' he said quietly, stepping back out of the doorway.

Emmie looked at the watch on her wrist - it now said 0:55. She nudged Jack and pointed at it, feeling her throat drying up. He took her hand in his and she could sense it tremble - the lack of time left was frightening.

The friends quickly walked along towards the forward staircase, reaching it through a pair of double doors. 'Just act natural and follow me,' Emmie whispered, as they emerged into the entrance hall. The queue was shorter here, and it felt like the floor had a greater slope - the increasing weight of water in the hull pulling the front end of the ship further down.

Emmie led Jack to join the back of the queue of passengers, slowly shuffling forward towards the stairs. They were fairly quiet - an air of despair and disbelief had settled over those lining up to be evacuated. When it was eventually their turn to ascend the staircase, they did so with a feeling of numbness - knowing that this was the final stage of the journey for so many people.

Coming up onto the deck above, Emmie glanced into what she took to be a 1st class lounge - heavily panelled and with large, comfortable chairs in. There were a surprising number of people still inside, given the queues leading up to the boat deck. She understood the context a few moments later, when a steward appeared, calling for women and children only.

'Guess the men have to stay and take their chances,' muttered Jack.

'That's society in 1912,' explained Emmie, 'chivalry is very much alive and well.' Her face darkened for a moment, 'Except where the 'lower' classes are concerned.' She was still shocked at how the class system of the day pervaded on board, and that the 3rd class passengers felt it right to sit and wait until given permission to save themselves.

The queue moved forward again, and up the final staircase to the boat deck. At the top of the steps, a steward was handing out lifejackets from a large stack on the floor. As Emmie and Jack put the linen vests over their heads and tied the strings together, it felt even more real. The presence of the cork-filled life preserver was a direct sign of their imminent departure from the ship and into the icy Atlantic.

'Put your blanket around your shoulders and then put the lifejacket on,' advised Emmie, helping Jack to re-tie his strings. 'We'll need every bit of warmth out there.' She shivered - the blankets were better than nothing, but there was no pretending it wasn't freezing beyond the large doors in the corner of the room.

They found out exactly how cold it was a few moments later, when they were called forward onto the deck outside. The chilled wind felt like it was slicing straight through them as it blew along the deck, and Emmie pulled the blanket tighter around her, in a futile attempt to keep it out.

Looking around them, the pair saw a scene wavering between efficient organisation and barely controlled chaos. Some of the lifeboats had already been launched and could be seen bobbing about in the dark sea below, their crewmen rowing clear of the doomed ship. The remaining lifeboats were where most of the chaos lay - it was obvious that the crew, whilst trying their best, were not altogether prepared for this outcome. Emmie watched one boat in particular being lowered at such an angle that the passengers inside were shouting in terror. There seemed to be no-one in overall charge, and those filing out of the doors onto the deck were loosely assigned a boat to queue for. In most cases, people waited quietly and followed the 'women and children first' protocol, but it was also possible to see passengers trying to push in. Emmie saw one man desperately offering handfuls of money to a crewman, in an attempt to be allowed onto a boat ahead of others. She wasn't sure whether to feel sorry for him or not - he was just scared after all, like everyone was.

Emmie looked across at the boat they had been directed to - there were an old couple standing by the edge, and the man was trying to encourage the woman to board the lifeboat. She recognised them as the people who had given her somewhere to sit earlier that evening. 'No,' the woman said, 'we've been together for many years, and I won't be separated from you now.' She stepped away from the boat and hugged her husband - 'Let others take our place - there are so many women and children on board still.'

A lump rose in Emmie's throat - this horrible situation was bringing out the best, and worst, in people. It was obvious that this couple knew they were unlikely to survive but were prepared to accept this for the benefit of others. She wiped a tear away and squeezed Jack's arm - 'This is so hard,' she said quietly, 'I never appreciated it would be this tragic.'

Jack looked at her - he had tears in his eyes too. It was hard not to, when faced with such a horrible set of events playing out all around you. 'Look,' he sniffed, pointing to a group of musicians who were filing out onto the deck - 'I always wondered if the stories about the band playing as the ship went down were true - seems that they are...' The musicians set up in a sheltered part of the deck alongside the entrance and began to play.

'Come forward, quickly please.' A steward was waving them towards the lifeboat they had been queuing for and Emmie took a few steps, then climbed up and over the side. The boat was already half full, and she squeezed onto one of the wooden benches which spanned the width of the vessel. As she sat down, she saw red distress flares being fired high up into the sky, casting an unnatural glow over the scene.

'Hurry up Jack,' she called, as he nervously swung his leg over the side to join her. It felt really high now they were sat in the lifeboat right on the edge of the deck. The boat was quite large in reality, but everything seemed small compared to the vast bulk of Titanic. Jack gripped hard onto the side as he sat down next to Emmie.

The lights on the deck flickered briefly, spooking the crewman who was stood in the rear of their boat. 'Lower away!' he shouted.

'But the boat's not full!' exclaimed Emmie, 'what about all of those people still on the deck?' She tried to stand up to make her point more strongly.

'Do you want to live or not?' said a woman next to her, tugging her back down again.

Emmie turned on her angrily - 'Those people need our help. It's selfish to just leave them.' The faces that she saw staring back at her from inside the boat ranged from impassive to downright scared. She could understand that but was enraged that there were still people who could be saved.

Looking around the boat again, something clicked inside Emmie's head - all of the passengers in the lifeboats were very well-dressed. Looking at Jack in horror, she cried out - 'Mary's not going to make it!'

'What do you mean?' he replied, still holding onto the edge of the boat.

'The 3rd class passengers aren't going to get a look in - they don't stand a chance!' She got to her feet, causing the boat to rock on the ropes it was suspended from.

'Sit down, miss,' ordered the crewman, 'you'll tip us over!'

'I'm getting off,' she said firmly, scrambling over Jack and swinging her leg over the edge of the lifeboat. As she reached the deck, she looked back and saw him frozen - unable to decide what to do. 'Now, Jack! Before it's too late!' She reached out a hand to him and watched him stand up, just as the boat started to be jerkily lowered. In the end, he almost rolled out as the edge of the boat descended past the deck.

Emmie bent down and pulled him to his feet, then led him away from the edge, saying quietly, 'It's ok,' over and over. Jack's face was ashen, and he was having difficulty holding it together. First, they were going home, then they were stuck in 1912 but hopefully safe, and now they were right back in harm's way.

It's Not About Us

Recognising that Jack was suffering from shock, Emmie tried to distract him by pointing to the musicians, who were trying their best with an upbeat number. Squinting, she suddenly nudged Jack - 'Hey - that looks like the busker from outside the tunnel!' One of the men playing violin did indeed bear a resemblance to the busker they had seen - or was it just the dinner suit and open overcoat that he was wearing?

'That's not possible, surely,' replied Jack shakily, trying to study the man's face. As the pair watched, the violinist turned and smiled at them, gently nodding his head.

'Maybe that's a sign,' whispered Emmie, 'if that was the busker, then perhaps we shouldn't give up hope after all. Jack smiled thinly - it felt like a lot to pin their hopes on...

'Can you move?' she asked, 'we've got to get to the back and see if we can do anything for Mary.'

'If we can find her...' Jack replied, taking a few tentative steps.

They half-ran, half-stumbled along the deck, dodging abandoned belongings and groups of disorientated passengers. All of the lifeboats on one side of Titanic had gone and, as they reached the end of the deck, they could see a large group of passengers huddled at the end, clearly not knowing what to do.

Emmie moved through the resigned mass of people and noticed that on the other side of the deck was a solitary lifeboat, hanging at an awkward angle in the ropes which held it. There were a couple of men trying unsuccessfully to right the boat - the ropes being badly twisted.

'Do you think we can help them?' suggested Jack, his shock at their plight having turned to denial.

Emmie was staring into the distance - 'I know who can,' she said quietly, taking off across the sloping deck and leaving Jack open-mouthed. He watched her run back into the crowd and emerge dragging John Kelly by the hand.

'Why are you still here? Why haven't you saved yourselves?' he said with surprise and concern.

'Don't worry about it now - can you help with that boat?' Emmie asked, pointing around the stairwell at the stranded lifeboat.

John Kelly ran across to the boat and looked at the tangle of ropes. He shook his head - 'I'm not sure we can do much.' Then, looking over the rail, he appeared to have an idea - 'The ship's sinking fast, and it won't be long before the water reaches the deck - I think we could cut the ropes then, and float it off.'

Emmie could hear the band still playing, even though the water level was so high - they had switched to a haunting melody which sounded familiar somehow.

Then everything happened at once - people appeared from all corners, trying to get a space on the last boat. Jack had to fight his way through the crowd to find Mary and the rest of the Kelly family, whilst John negotiated room on board for them.

Mary arrived with her mother and siblings, chilled through, and having almost given up hope. She gave Emmie and Jack a quick hug of thanks before her father bundled them into the lifeboat, along with as many others as he dared. They watched the sea rise ever closer - he and another man standing in the boat with knives drawn, ready to cut the ropes at the right moment.

'Now!' Mary's father shouted, feeling the lifeboat rock as the waves touched the bottom. There was a large splash and the boat dropped, settling safely onto the surface.

'What now?' sniffed Jack, frantically chewing his lip and looking around in fright. 'That's it - there's no more boats. We're going to drown!'

'No we're not,' said Emmie firmly, though she was terrified too and had no plan for their salvation. 'All we can do is get as far back as possible and hope - the time architect told us that we would get home if we helped Mary.'

Jack shook his head back and forth - 'He was wrong - face it.' He did, however, allow himself to be led back up the deck towards the stairwell. They quickly clattered down a couple of levels, emerging onto the small deck near the general room. Next, they climbed almost vertically to reach the poop deck which, was now suspended high out of the water.

As they fought their way up the steeply sloping deck, using the side rail as support, the scene around them was total carnage. There were people clinging onto benches, and others jumping into the icy water. A few unfortunate passengers lost their footing and fell down the steep deck, onto the sinking part of the ship.

Hauling themselves to the rear rail, Emmie and Jack could go no further. This was it - the ship was going down and, in a matter of minutes, even their current perch would disappear beneath the waves. The remaining lights on board flickered and went out, causing screams from some of the passengers still clinging on.

Gritting her teeth and holding onto the rail tightly, Emmie put out a hand to Jack. He gave it a squeeze and let out a loud sob, just as there was an unearthly creaking sound and the rear section they were on tipped fully vertical, leaving them facing straight down at the sea.

'Aargh!' cried Emmie, unable to hold on against the pull of gravity any longer. Jack managed a split second more - just long enough for him to hear the alarm on Emmie's watch start to sound, as she disappeared from sight.

He braced for the impact, hoping that it would be quick. When it came, the breath was knocked out of him and he lay there for a second, wondering why he wasn't wet. The distress of seeing Emmie fall in front of him had convulsed his body with grief, and he wasn't really aware of his surroundings.

'Jack?' came a quiet voice at his side. It sounded like Emmie, and he tried to block it out because it was too painful. He didn't know what was going on, but he had seen her fall into the foaming sea in front of him. 'Jack...?' the voice came again - this time he put his hands over his ears to stop hearing it. In doing so, he scraped his knuckles on something hard, and looked around in confusion.

Why was there a wall in the sea? He reached out and touched it - confirming that it definitely felt like a wall. Was he dead? Was this what being dead was like?

Something prodded him in the side, and he jerked around to look - now Emmie was looking at him! He screwed his eyes up, then opened them again. She was still there, and now she was speaking to him again.

Eventually, he gave in to his mind and answered her. 'Where are we...?'

'At last!' she cried, 'I thought you'd lost the plot...!' He sat up and she hugged him, both crying with the emotion which was coursing through their bodies.

'This is the tunnel, isn't it? We must have made it - just like the man said.'

Emmie sniffed the air - there was a damp, fusty note which had replaced the salty tang of the sea. 'I think it is!' She grabbed his hand and pulled him to his feet. Each could feel the other shaking with relief at their unexpected and lucky escape.

'I really thought if we survived, that we were going to be in 1912 forever,' said Jack, wiping his face.

'I'll be honest, I didn't think we were going to make it,' Emmie admitted.

He turned to her - 'Come on, let's get back to the others before we're missed. Hopefully time hasn't passed in the present...'

'I do hope Mary and her family made it,' said Emmie, as they walked slowly along the tunnel in the direction of the light.

'Me too,' agreed Jack quietly, 'for everyone's sake, including ours.'

As they emerged from the tunnel entrance, Emmie glanced towards the shop front to her left. The busker had gone, though somewhat appropriately there was now a large puddle of water where he had previously stood.

To their immense relief, Mr Hughes was still explaining the intricacies of fitting out Titanic in the dry dock, when they slipped back into the group of students. 'It's hard to imagine how ornate the interior must have looked,' he said importantly. 'Of course, there are some photos, but they struggle to convey the scale of the grandeur...'

Emmie nudged Jack - 'If only he knew...' she whispered with a smile.

All For Something

A few weeks later, Jack and Emmie were back at school and working on an assignment. It was about family trees and how to use historical records to trace your ancestors. They had been asked to use an ancestry website to investigate their own families and see what information they could unearth.

'I reckon if I go back far enough, I'll find a pirate in my family,' said Jack with a grin. 'Ooh arr!'

Emmie looked across at him from the next computer workstation - 'That's wishful thinking I imagine...' She clicked on a few more records, before adding - 'We'll probably both find we're descended from fishermen, or something traditional like that.'

'You just wait and see,' retorted Jack, 'there'll be some sort of surprise - I can feel it.'

'This is interesting.' Emmie interrupted Jack's flow, beckoning him over. 'It looks like one of my ancestors joined the Navy.' Up on the screen was a service record for a Samuel Langford, filled in with neat, looping handwriting.

Jack looked at the screen - '1876,' he said, 'that's a long time ago.' The record was for the merchant navy - sailors who worked on ships carrying cargo around the world. 'I wonder what kind of exciting places he might have visited.'

'This looks to be the dates of when he enlisted, got promoted and eventually retired,' Emmie mused, 'I wonder if I can find anything out about the ships he was on, and where they went?'

'Hold on a minute,' exclaimed Jack, 'see when he retired - 1912, and look - he worked for Cunard at the time. That's when Titanic sank, isn't it? Maybe he got a chance to see her?'

'Maybe...' replied Emmie, thinking for a moment, then typing quickly on the keyboard.

'What are you doing?' Jack asked.

'Well, you saying about Titanic reminded me about Mary and her family. I wondered if we could find out what happened to them.'

Jack looked serious for a moment - they'd spoken about little other than their Titanic experience since returning, but the close shave both felt at actually getting home in one piece was a bit raw still. 'I hope they made it...' he said quietly. 'Then again - the world is still pretty normal, so I guess we fixed time after all.'

Emmie typed away for a few more minutes, alternating with the mouse and keyboard to navigate the various websites they had been shown previously. 'Aha!' she said suddenly - 'Titanic survivor lists...' Her finger hovered over the mouse button - unsure whether to actually press it. 'Do you want to know?' she asked, turning to Jack, 'what if it's bad news?'

'If it is, it's already happened - we can't change it now.'

'Ok,' Emmie pressed the button and started scanning down the list, 'J... K... Kelly!' She ran her finger down the screen, holding her breath as she passed numerous people with the surname. 'Mary,' she said, stopping at two entries for 'Kelly, Mary'.

'Which is it?' Jack asked, looking over her shoulder. 'Did she ever say where she was from in Ireland?'

'I can't remember,' admitted Emmie, 'but look - there's a John Kelly, no - wait, there's two John Kelly's listed from the same place as this top entry for Mary...'

'That must be them - try Patrick too,' suggested Jack. Before long, the pair had established which of the Kelly passengers on the list had been part of Mary's family. 'Just need to scroll across and see what happened to them now.'

Emmie slowly dragged the scroll bar to the side, breathing out with relief as the word 'Rescued' appeared next to Mary's name. She quickly scanned up and down the list, checking the other members of the Kelly family and finding that they had all been rescued too. Switching to a search engine, she typed Mary's name in, then stared at the screen in shocked surprise. 'It says here that a Mary Kelly was instrumental in the production of penicillin in the 1940's. Apparently, her work saved countless lives in the Second World War.'

'Let me see?' said Jack, intrigued that the small girl they had known might have gone onto such great things. He leaned over Emmie and moved the mouse around - below the headline was a black and white photo of a middle-aged woman in a laboratory.

'That's Mary!' said Emmie excitedly - although thirty years must have passed, she was still recognisable to them. A rush of emotion hit her as she turned to Jack, two large tears rolling down her cheeks.

'Hey, come here,' he said, putting an arm around her - 'it worked out in the end, and it was all down to you. If you hadn't been so determined to help, then we might not be seeing those words on the screen today. I'm sure they had a long and happy life, thanks to your kindness.'

Emmie squeezed Jack back and allowed herself a little feeling of satisfaction - the consequences of their first adventure in time had been put right in the second. 'Do you ever wonder why all of this happened to us?' she asked, 'I'd like to find out some day...'

For The Curious...

Discovering Titanic

Almost as soon as Titanic sank, there were proposals for how to raise her from the ocean floor. Some of these were very unusual and included pumping the hull full of Vaseline or filling it with millions of ping pong balls! The depth to which Titanic had sunk proved a major problem too - at around 3,800 metres, this was far beyond the reach of divers of the day.

In 1985, an American oceanographer called Robert Ballard, proposed a new approach to finding Titanic. Several previous attempts had been made using sonar to discover the wreck itself, but Ballard used the cameras on a deep-water remote vehicle to look for the debris field instead. He had experienced other shipwrecks where parts of the ship had been scattered far and wide on the way to the bottom and knew that the debris would cover a far larger area than the wreck itself.

On 1st September 1985, pieces of debris began to appear on screens within the research vessel operating the underwater camera. One was identified as a boiler, which could be matched to pictures taken during Titanic's construction. The wreck had finally been found.

The Last Survivor to Leave Titanic

Titanic's chief baker - Charles Joughin - is widely thought to be the last person to get off the ship as it sank.

He had been helping to load passengers into lifeboats, and once the boats were all full, threw a large number of deckchairs overboard so that people in the sea could use them to float on.

He finally found himself on the poop deck, at the rear of the ship, holding onto the safety rail around the edge. As Titanic tipped steeply, the stern raised out of the water, and Charles Joughin was able to descend with the sinking ship like he was in a lift, stepping into the water with barely a splash.

He survived several hours treading water in the sea, until he saw a lifeboat as dawn broke. He was rescued with his only injuries being swollen feet.

The 'Lucky' Fireman

John Coffey was a 23-year-old fireman on Titanic, who lived in Cobh, Ireland (then known as Queenstown). His job was to shovel coal into the huge boilers which powered the ship, and it was back-breaking work. He set sail from Southampton on Titanic, having previously sailed on her sister ship, Olympic. He was homesick and wanted to see his family.

As Titanic steamed into Queenstown, her last stop before crossing the Atlantic, John put his plan into action. The ship was too large to berth at the quayside, so passengers and mail had to be ferried out on small boats. John crept onto a boat carrying mail and hid himself beneath the pile of sacks. As the boat arrived in the harbour, he was able to slip ashore without being seen.

There is some debate as to whether John Coffey had always intended to abscond from Titanic to see his family, or whether, as he claimed later, he had a strange foreboding about the voyage which made him uneasy.

Whatever the truth may have been, John Coffey has to be regarded as having a lucky escape from the famous ship.

About The Author

Glen Blackwell lives in Suffolk, England. He has a career in finance and *The Titanic Tunnel* is his third book. Inspired by bedtime reading with his 3 daughters, Glen loves to bring stories to life for young readers.

Glen would love to hear what you thought about *The Titanic Tunnel* - please contact him as below:

www.glenblackwell.com

Facebook.com/glenblackwellauthor

Twitter: @gblackwellbooks

Instagram: @gblackwellbooks

Alternatively, please leave a review on Amazon or your favourite online bookstore so that other readers can see what you thought.

Thank you!

Readers' Club

It would be great if you would like to join Glen's Readers' Club. Sign up to receive a free eBook at **www.glenblackwell.com/readersclub**

You will also be the first to hear about Glen's new books and get the chance to become an advance reader for new titles.

If you are under 13 then please ask an adult to sign up for you.

Follow Glen

Facebook.com/glenblackwellauthor

Twitter: @gblackwellbooks

Instagram: @gblackwellbooks

Join Jack & Emmie on The Blitz Bus